Man Killer

Once the bear caught sight of Clint and Ordell, it thundered toward them more powerfully than ever.

"Just stay where you are," Ordell said under his breath as the ground beneath him shook with the approaching bear's steps.

Clint leaned against the tree and watched the bear draw closer.

Ordell let out a slow breath and squeezed his trigger. His rifle let out a single blast, which rolled through the air like a clap of thunder. The barrel jumped up, kicking Ordell on the shoulder as black smoke poured from one end.

The bear kept running toward the tree as Ordell slowly lowered his rifle. He didn't even bother going through the motions of reloading the weapon since he and Clint would both be killed three times over before he was halfway done.

Clint leaned back and gritted his teeth. At that moment, he saw the cold emptiness in the bear's eyes . . .

DON'T MISS THESE
ALL-ACTION WESTERN SERIES
FROM THE BERKLEY PUBLISHING GROUP

THE GUNSMITH by J. R. Roberts
Clint Adams was a legend among lawmen, outlaws, and ladies. They called him . . . the Gunsmith.

LONGARM by Tabor Evans
The popular long-running series about Deputy U.S. Marshal Long—his life, his loves, his fight for justice.

SLOCUM by Jake Logan
Today's longest-running action Western. John Slocum rides a deadly trail of hot blood and cold steel.

BUSHWHACKERS by B. J. Lanagan
An action-packed series by the creators of Longarm! The rousing adventures of the most brutal gang of cutthroats ever assembled—Quantrill's Raiders.

DIAMONDBACK by Guy Brewer
Dex Yancey is Diamondback, a Southern gentleman turned con man when his brother cheats him out of the family fortune. Ladies love him. Gamblers hate him. But nobody pulls one over on Dex . . .

WILDGUN by Jack Hanson
The blazing adventures of mountain man Will Barlow—from the creators of Longarm!

TEXAS TRACKER by Tom Calhoun
Meet J.T. Law: the most relentless—and dangerous—manhunter in all Texas. Where sheriffs and posses fail, he's the best man to bring in the most vicious outlaws—for a price.

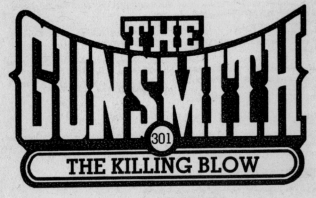

THE GUNSMITH

301

THE KILLING BLOW

J. R. ROBERTS

J

JOVE BOOKS, NEW YORK

THE BERKLEY PUBLISHING GROUP
Published by the Penguin Group
Penguin Group (USA) Inc.
375 Hudson Street, New York, New York 10014, USA
Penguin Group (Canada), 90 Eglinton Avenue East, Suite 700, Toronto, Ontario M4P 2Y3, Canada
(a division of Pearson Penguin Canada Inc.)
Penguin Books Ltd., 80 Strand, London WC2R 0RL, England
Penguin Group Ireland, 25 St. Stephen's Green, Dublin 2, Ireland (a division of Penguin Books Ltd.)
Penguin Group (Australia), 250 Camberwell Road, Camberwell, Victoria 3124, Australia
(a division of Pearson Australia Group Pty. Ltd.)
Penguin Books India Pvt. Ltd., 11 Community Centre, Panchsheel Park, New Delhi—110 017, India
Penguin Group (NZ), Cnr. Airborne and Rosedale Roads, Albany, Auckland 1310, New Zealand
(a division of Pearson New Zealand Ltd.)
Penguin Books (South Africa) (Pty.) Ltd., 24 Sturdee Avenue, Rosebank, Johannesburg 2196,
South Africa

Penguin Books Ltd., Registered Offices: 80 Strand, London WC2R 0RL, England

This is a work of fiction. Names, characters, places, and incidents either are the product of the author's imagination or are used fictitiously, and any resemblance to actual persons, living or dead, business establishments, events, or locales is entirely coincidental.

THE KILLING BLOW

A Jove Book / published by arrangement with the author

PRINTING HISTORY
Jove edition / January 2007

ISBN: 978-0-515-14244-0

JOVE®
Jove Books are published by The Berkley Publishing Group,
a division of Penguin Group (USA) Inc.,
375 Hudson Street, New York, New York 10014.
JOVE is a registered trademark of Penguin Group (USA) Inc.
The "J" design is a trademark belonging to Penguin Group (USA) Inc.

PRINTED IN THE UNITED STATES OF AMERICA

10 9 8 7 6 5 4 3 2 1

ONE

Clint brought the rifle up to his shoulder and sighted along the top of the barrel. Although his heart was pounding in his chest so hard that it made his eyes waver a bit, he did his best to push through that and stay focused on the task at hand.

There wasn't any room to make a mistake. Even a small one. When he pulled his trigger, he needed to do it at the right time and with just the right amount of pressure. Otherwise, he could make a mistake. Considering the fact that there was a black bear at the other end of his barrel, Clint knew he couldn't afford to make many mistakes.

Even waiting for half a second too long might be enough to get his throat opened and every limb torn from his body.

Clint pulled his trigger and felt the rifle kick against his shoulder.

The bear howled angrily and shuddered as the hot lead thumped into his chest. Although he staggered for a moment, the bear recovered as quickly as if he'd just been stung by a bee and wheeled around to get a look at where that bee had come from.

"Damn," Clint muttered under his breath as he levered in another round.

He'd seen more than his share of tense moments, many of which had forced him to look straight down the wrong end of a gun barrel. None of those moments, however, sent a chill under Clint's skin as when he saw that bear look straight at him and let out a hungry roar.

As much as he tried to keep his movements steady, Clint couldn't help but take his next shot in a hurry. The bear had started moving toward him, picking up speed like a boulder rolling down the side of a mountain, moving unbelievably fast for something that size.

It seemed to take forever for the rifle's lever to complete its short set of movements. When Clint heard the mechanism click into place, he aimed from the hip and pulled the rifle's trigger again.

The bear had just launched the front half of its body into the air after slamming its front paws against the packed earth. While still moving forward like a derailed train, it reared halfway up and splayed out its forepaws to show Clint the huge claws that were about to rip him into pieces.

With his second shot still ringing in his ears, Clint worked the lever and fired again. He could barely hear the shot, but he could see a patch of the bear's fur twitch as hot lead thumped into a wall of solid muscle.

Clint's reflexes were barely sharp enough to cut through his instinctual panic and get his entire body moving to one side. He pushed off with both legs, not caring where he was going or how gracefully he could get there. All he wanted to do was get away from those incoming claws before he felt them up close and personally.

Although Clint wasn't able to land on his legs or outstretched arms, he managed to avoid those claws. The bear's paws slammed in quick succession against the ground, sending tremors through the dirt right beneath Clint's body.

Suddenly, a scream pierced the air.

For a moment, Clint wasn't even aware of the noise since the blood was coursing so powerfully through his head. The bear heard it, which was enough to divert its attention just long enough for Clint to roll another few yards away from the angry beast.

When he righted himself, Clint took a quick breath and looked in the direction of those screams. The woman was still in the same spot she'd been when Clint had first spotted her: huddled against an overturned wagon with her arms wrapped around a small child. Her dress was torn off one shoulder and her face was smeared with dirt as well as a bit of blood. The child appeared to be a boy, but Clint couldn't be certain since the little one's face was buried in the woman's arms.

It had only been a few minutes since Clint had arrived at the clearing where the wagon had overturned, but it seemed like years ago. Of course, with the huge black bear coming at him like a monster from a bad dream, a man tended to savor every second as if it were his last.

"Get away from there!" Clint shouted.

The sound of the woman's desperate breathing could be heard even over the bear's snarls and the rush of blood through Clint's ears. She looked back and forth between Clint and the bear, only to stay where she was and clutch her child even tighter.

"I can't . . ." she gasped. "I can't move."

"Think about that child and get moving," Clint shouted. "I can help, but not if you're too scared to move."

"I can't move," she repeated. "The wagon's pinning me down."

The bear was on all fours, swaying its head back and forth to look at the people around him. Although the talking seemed to be distracting it for the moment, the animal's patience was obviously wearing thin.

Clint got back to his feet and took a moment to replace the spent ammunition in his rifle. Patting his side quickly was enough to tell him that his modified Colt was still right where it should be. Craning his neck to get a better look at the woman, Clint saw the spot where the frame of the wagon was leaning down on top of her leg.

As if picking up on the scent of the woman's fear, the bear turned more in her direction and lowered its head while stalking forward. Each step made a heavy crunching sound as branches and rocks were ground beneath its weight. Lines of saliva started dripping from the corners of its mouth as rumbling breaths issued from within its massive frame.

At that moment, as if she were reading the worst fears going through Clint's mind, the woman started kicking and batting at the wagon in a flurry of motion. Even though he was no expert on animals, Clint figured that was the worst possible thing she could have done.

He was right.

The bear let out an aggressive snarl and reared up in response to the movement it saw. While it was still on its hind legs and pawing at the sky, another stinging pain lanced through its torso.

Clint fired off a shot from his rifle and followed it up with another one. "Come on you big bastard!" he shouted. "Look over here!"

The bear's roar took on a bit of a pained tone, but that was pretty much the only reaction it gave to being shot. As far as the bullet wounds were concerned, all Clint could see were some slick spots in the bear's fur.

Since the woman didn't look like she was going to tire out or stop trying to get free anytime soon, Clint pulled in a breath, put all common sense aside and ran into the bear's field of vision. After waving his arms a bit, Clint saw the bear's massive head swing toward him as the animal's eyes locked onto this new distraction.

"That's it," Clint said. "Come to me."

And that's exactly what the bear did.

In fact, the bear rushed toward Clint so quickly that it forced Clint to fire his next shot wildly past the bear's head rather than through it. Hearing the angry hiss of that bullet whip past its ear stoked the fire in the bear's belly and got it thundering toward Clint with renewed vigor.

Even though Clint's mind was telling him to take another shot and put the bear down, every muscle in his body was telling him to run.

And so he ran.

Clint ran faster than he'd ever thought possible.

Even with his legs pumping furiously beneath him and the wind whistling through his ears, he started to doubt if it would be enough.

TWO

Clint's first thought was to get the bear away from the woman and her child. Now that he'd accomplished that much, Clint was just trying to stay alive as he bolted for the trees with the bear hot on his heels.

Having left the trail behind him, Clint found himself in a thick tangle of trees and fallen logs. If he wasn't jumping to one side to avoid one, he was forced to jump at odd intervals to avoid the other. All the while, the bear plowed through everything in its path as it stormed closer and closer to Clint's back.

Suddenly, Clint felt himself getting pulled off balance. He thought he'd gotten his foot caught under something or twisted his knee, but quickly realized he was literally being pulled. The hand that had clamped onto his shoulder was nearly as big as the bear's paw and it yanked Clint to one side like a child picking up a rag doll.

The bear let out a growl and stomped past the big tree where Clint and another man were now hiding.

"You don't hunt bears much, do you mister?" the other man asked.

Clint took a moment to catch his breath and get a look at where he was. He'd been pulled behind a tree that was

6

just thick enough to keep from being knocked over by the rampaging bear. Leaning against the trunk, wearing an amused grin on his face, was a man who seemed to be just as scarred as the battered tree itself.

The man looked to be in his late fifties, but could have actually been ten years in either direction of that age. He was barrel-chested and wore thick layers of tanned hides on his back, which were crudely held together by leather laces.

Grinning through a thick layer of gray beard, the man nodded a quick greeting to Clint before letting go of his shoulder and tipping his hat. "Name's Mark Ordell. You after that big fella?"

"No," Clint said. "Just trying to get it away from some folks back there trapped under an overturned wagon."

Ordell craned his neck to look around the tree. He barely seemed to notice the angry snarls of the bear as it skidded on the ground and struggled to get its massive frame turned back around. "Oh, I see it," Ordell said. "You know them folks?"

"No, I just—"

"Then you must've ridden in on that black Darley Arabian over there. That's one hell of a nice horse."

"Do you know that bear's coming back?"

"Oh, sure. It'll take it a little while to get situated and then catch sight of us, though. That's why you shouldn't run away from a monster like that in a straight line. Damn thing could outrun a stagecoach once it gets moving."

"Very interesting," Clint said. "Do you have a good way to kill it?"

Ordell grinned and nodded as he lifted a rifle so caked with dirt it resembled a tree branch. "I believe I've got just the thing."

The bear loped in a circle less than ten paces from the tree where Clint and Ordell were hiding. Its eyes were still flaring with rage and every one of its moves were filled with raw power.

"That there's not just any bear," Ordell said as he raised his rifle and placed its narrow stock against his shoulder. "He's famous."

Even though Clint wasn't a trapper by trade, he knew every kind of rifle that had been made. The one in Ordell's hands wasn't anything that could be bought in a store. It was most definitely cobbled together from some very old pieces.

"You're a trapper?" Clint asked.

Sighting along a barrel that was longer than Clint's arm, Ordell said, "Yes, sir."

"And you're after that bear?"

"Yep."

"Any reason why you couldn't have shot it before it nearly killed me as well as that woman and her child?"

The grin hadn't disappeared from the older man's face, but it did widen a bit as he leaned against the stock of his rifle. "Because I didn't know exactly where he was until you were kind enough to get him to holler for me."

"Glad to be a help."

"You want to help again? Why don't you take another shot at him with that pop gun of yours?"

Clint looked down at the rifle as if making sure that's what the older man was referring to. Actually, compared to the oversized musket in Ordell's hands, Clint's rifle did resemble a toy. "I already tried it," Clint said. "You saw how well that worked. You've got to be more ready for this than I am."

"True enough, but I only got one shot at a time. That means I kind of need to make them count."

Clint couldn't take his eyes away from the bear as it lumbered to bring itself around and sniff hungrily at the air. For the moment, its attention seemed to be focused on the spot Clint should have been instead of where he was.

"You folks are luckier than most," Ordell said in a quiet, almost reverent voice. "That bear's been known to sneak up and pounce like a damn cat. I guess that wagon turning over must've spooked him."

"I just can't take the chance of it coming back. There's a lady back there who's hurt."

"He won't be coming back," Ordell said. "Not if I can help it."

"Then go ahead and take your shot."

"After you, my friend. All I need is to catch the big fella's attention."

Shrugging, Clint brought the rifle up, aimed and fired. It sent a bullet into the bear's side, causing it to stagger and turn toward the tree. For a second, it looked as if all those previous rifle shots had finally added up to do some damage. Then, once the bear caught sight of Clint and Ordell, it thundered toward them more powerfully than ever.

"Just stay where you are," Ordell said under his breath as the ground beneath him shook with the approaching bear's steps.

Clint leaned against the tree and watched the bear draw closer. "Any day now," he grunted.

Ordell let out a slow breath and squeezed his trigger. His rifle let out a single blast, which rolled through the air like a clap of thunder. The barrel jumped up, kicking Ordell on the shoulder as black smoke poured from one end.

Clint could hear something that almost sounded like a hammer thumping against a wet board.

The bear kept running toward the tree as Ordell slowly lowered his rifle. He didn't even bother going through the motions of reloading the weapon since he and Clint would both be killed three times over before he was halfway done.

Clint leaned back and gritted his teeth. At that moment, he saw the cold emptiness in the bear's eyes.

After taking one more step, the bear simply dropped down and let its own momentum drive its head into the ground. Its paws were still ripping at the dirt, but weren't strong enough to support its own weight. After a few more kicks, the bear let out a final growl and then stopped moving.

Only then did Clint realize his shoulders were up around his ears and that he hadn't taken a full breath since he'd first climbed down from Eclipse's saddle.

Ordell, on the other hand, looked like he was posing for a photograph. With his rifle in one hand like a walking stick, he leaned forward and nodded slowly. Glancing over to Clint, he said, "That wasn't so hard, now was it?"

THREE

When Clint and Ordell walked back to the overturned wagon, they heard the woman yelp a bit as if she'd seen the bear return. When she spotted the two men instead of the single animal, she let out a relieved sigh.

"Who's that?" she asked.

Clint knelt down beside the wagon and said, "He's the man who killed that bear."

"I figure we'll all be eating real good tonight," Ordell said.

"I can think about food once I get this wagon off of me."

Clint reached under the wagon and found the spot where her leg was pinned. "Can you feel that?"

She nodded.

"And does it hurt?"

Ordell laughed under his breath and said, "If she ain't hollering her lungs out, then she's just fine."

Looking to Clint, she said, "It does hurt a bit, but I should be all right."

"See? I told ya."

"All right then, doctor," Clint said. "Do you think you can help me lift this wagon?"

Ordell leaned his rifle against the nearest tree and

11

peeled the tattered coat from his shoulders. He then spat on both his callused palms, rubbed them together and took a firm grip upon the edge of the wagon. "Ready when you are."

Positioning himself next to Ordell, Clint took hold of the wagon and looked to the woman before lifting. "Can you pull your leg out on your own?"

"If it means getting out from under here, I'll drag myself all the way back to Georgia," she replied.

Clint nodded and looked over to Ordell. "On three. One. Two. Three."

Even with both men straining every muscle in their arms, back and shoulders, the wagon only moved enough for the woman to pull herself out about an inch. Her eyes widened and she scooted back where she was the moment she felt the wagon coming down again.

"My knee's stuck," she said. "I have to get it all out or nothing."

"Think you can lift this thing any higher?" Ordell asked.

After catching his breath, Clint looked over to the closest tree. "I've got a better idea."

The instant he saw Clint walk over and take the rifle that had been leaning against that tree, Ordell jumped to his feet. "Just what the hell do you think you're gonna do with that?"

"Use it to give us a little leverage."

"Why don't you use yer own damn rifle for that?"

"Because my rifle isn't a solid iron tree trunk that's almost as tall as I am. That gun's strong enough to last through doomsday, so it's strong enough to get that wagon off the lady's knee. If you can find something else that can do the trick, be my guest."

After taking a quick look around, Ordell grumbled under his breath and reclaimed his rifle. "At least let me do it."

"All right. I'll get back and lift to make it as easy on that gun as possible."

Even though Clint had made the offer jokingly, Ordell looked as if he were seriously considering sacrificing his firstborn child. He took hold of his rifle by the stock and then wedged the barrel under one corner of the wagon. The first time he pulled on the rifle, Ordell did so halfheartedly at best. Once he saw Clint straining and the lady struggling, he put more of his back into it.

Before too long, the wagon groaned as it shifted from the spot where it had been wedged into the ground. Beads of sweat poured down both men's faces until finally the wagon shifted again and the lady squirmed free from beneath it.

Until now, the child in her arms had been so quiet and so still that Clint had almost forgotten it was there. Once the lady was able to get out from under the wagon, however, the child popped from her arms and scurried away.

"Looks like the boy's gonna be all right," Ordell said.

Clint kept his eyes on the boy and took his first good look at him. Although the boy's face was smudged with dirt and his clothes were ripped in a few spots, he moved just fine. He looked back at Clint with a little bit of nervousness in his eyes, but he still looked alert.

"You all right?" Clint asked.

The boy nodded and then scurried back to the lady, who wrapped her arms around him and pressed her face against the top of his head.

Shifting his eyes toward the lady, Clint asked, "What about you? Can you get up?"

"I'm not sure." Before Clint or Ordell could get close enough to her to help, she tried getting her legs beneath her. She winced with pain a few times, and nearly fell over when she actually tried to stand. When she attempted it again, she had a man on each arm to help her up.

Clint and Ordell brought the woman slowly to her feet and held her up rather than allowing her to support her own full weight. Together, they lowered her down a bit and picked her up again when they heard her pull in a sharp, pained breath.

"We need to get a better look at that leg," Clint said.

Ordell eased away from her once he saw that the lady was naturally leaning more toward Clint. "Then I might as well gather some wood and set up camp."

"Camp?" the lady asked. "But we need to get moving again. We're expected in Westerlake."

"Where's Westerlake?" Clint asked.

"Oregon."

"That'd normally be another day's ride, but this isn't exactly normal."

"My son and I need to get there. Otherwise my family will worry."

"And it seems they'd be right to worry," Clint pointed out. "Especially since we were nearly killed by a bear—"

"Speak for yerself," Ordell muttered.

Clint tossed the rifle he'd borrowed into Ordell's hands. "Most of us almost got killed by a bear," Clint corrected. "And some of us don't have a wagon anymore."

"The horses should still be around here," the lady said while looking around in every direction. "Somewhere."

"And we should find them before long. Right now, it's getting dark and we all could use a rest." Holding a hand toward Ordell, Clint added, "Most of us do. We can get a fresh start in the morning. How's that?"

By now, the lady's breathing had calmed and she nodded warily. "If you wouldn't mind staying with us, I'd appreciate it."

"My pleasure," Clint said. "Although I can't speak for my trapper friend over there."

Ordell was already wandering back into the trees with his rifle over his shoulder. "I intend on stuffing my gourd with fresh bear meat tonight. If you folks intend on building a good-sized cooking fire, I don't mind sharing."

Clint made sure the lady was situated and then rubbed his hands together. "All right, then. Looks like we've got ourselves a picnic."

FOUR

It wasn't long before the sun was on its way down, but the shadows grew long way before that. The spot where Clint and Ordell set up the camp was a little ways off the trail and nestled within a thick batch of trees. The remains of the bear had been covered with enough dirt to keep the smell away, but the remains of the wagon weren't so easy to hide.

Half of the cart had been splintered and damaged beyond repair. The other half had been stripped away and the wood was put to plenty of other uses. One of those was to feed the large fire that was blazing brightly in the middle of a stone circle. Large chunks of meat were stretched over the flames, filling the air with the mouth-watering scent of dinner.

Clint walked into the camp, leading three horses by their reins. One of them was his own Darley Arabian stallion. Another belonged to Ordell and the third was still twitchy and jumping at every snap and crackle coming from the campfire.

"Where's Petey?" the lady asked.

Clint looked around and immediately spotted the young boy, so he figured that wasn't the child's name. "Petey?"

16

"The other horse," she said. "He's a dark gray with—"

"Oh, the horse," Clint said. "He was hurt pretty badly."

"But I saw him run away once the harness was broken."

"He didn't make it far. I found him with one broken leg and another that looked pretty twisted up. I had to . . . uh . . ." When he saw the child looking directly at him, Clint started struggling for a more delicate choice of words.

"You had to shoot him," the boy said, beating Clint to the punch. Looking to the lady, he added, "It's best that way, you know."

"Yes, sweetie," she replied while rubbing the top of the boy's head. "I know."

Clint sat down at the edge of the fire and nodded to Ordell. The bigger man was sitting on a stump and leaning toward the fire so he could tend to the cooking. The lady and the young boy were on the opposite side of the fire.

Now that there weren't any wild animals about or wagons that needed to be lifted, Clint actually had a moment to get a close look at the two folks who'd called him onto this section of trail in the first place.

The boy looked to be somewhere between eight and ten years old. He had bright blond hair and even brighter blue eyes. Although the blood had been wiped from his face, he still wore his ripped jacket proudly as if mimicking the tattered appearance of the big man cooking the bear meat. Despite weighing less than one of the wagon's busted wheels, the boy held up pretty well after the crash and ensuing bear attack. In fact, the little guy seemed to be enjoying himself as if this were just another camping trip.

The woman had darker blond hair and a slightly darker hue to her skin. Part of that seemed to come from the sun, but there was also something else that gave her a naturally exotic look. Her dark brown eyes smoldered like embers in the fire and her soft lips had yet to curl up into a smile.

"Now that I know the horse's name," Clint said, "perhaps I should know yours."

Finally, the lady smiled and she lowered her head as a blush found its way onto her cheeks. "It's Allison Stapp. This is my son."

"Joseph," the boy said, beating her to the punch. He stood up straight and stuck his hand out toward Clint.

"Clint Adams," he said while shaking the boy's hand. "Pleased to meet you."

When he saw the Stapps looking in his direction, the bigger man leaning toward the fire said, "Mark Ordell."

"Normally, I'm more mindful of my manners," Allison said.

"You from Georgia?" Ordell asked.

"Why yes. How'd you know?"

"Georgia girls have the prettiest accent there is."

Maintaining her blush, Allison averted her eyes and wound up looking toward Clint.

Rather than try to ease her embarrassment, Clint simply shrugged and said, "It's true."

She nodded and sat up since she wasn't about to get much comfort from anyone around that fire. "Thank you," she said.

Ordell chuckled and nodded appreciatively. "And there it is. Sweet as honey."

Both men laughed as Allison picked up a pebble and tossed it at Ordell. When she got up, Allison curtsied and spoke like she was the belle of the ball. "If you gentlemen don't mind, ah'd like to freshen up a bit. Ah do believe there's a lake nearby."

After watching her leave, Ordell shifted back around and prodded the bear meat sizzling over the flames.

"You said that bear was famous," Clint remarked. "What did you mean?"

"It's a man killer, is what I mean. Took out a bunch of men at a lumber camp a few miles from here as well as a few . . ." He paused and shot a quick glance toward Joseph. "As well as a few others at a house up in the hills."

Clint nodded. "I suppose there's a reward for the hide?"

"Yep."

"I can help you clean up the carcass and stretch out that hide, then."

Ordell narrowed his eyes a bit and asked, "You expectin' a piece of the reward?"

"After I went through the trouble of flushing him out and running him straight to you?" Clint asked indignantly. "Actually, no. After all you've done, I thought I could lend you a hand as a way to say thanks. The reward's all yours. You earned it."

"If you want to thank me, you'd fix the damage you caused to my baby."

"Huh?"

"My rifle," Ordell said as he reached over, picked up the huge weapon and tossed it to Clint. "See for yourself."

Clint caught the rifle with both hands and immediately felt the imperfection in the way it felt. The weapon resembled a musket at first, but the hammer and firing mechanism were much more up-to-date. The stock had obviously been around for a long time and was marred by notches and other markings all up and down the wooden surface.

Although those parts of the gun caught Clint's professional interest, it was the barrel that immediately caused his hackles to rise. The thick iron was bored out and the rest was thickened to accommodate the work. Despite the sturdiness of the iron, however, being used as a lever was enough to put a nasty bend a quarter of the way down from the sights.

"What caliber is this?" Clint asked.

"Fifty-two," Ordell said proudly. "I made it myself and I make the ammunition as well. None of that matters if the damn barrel is bent worse than a pig's pecker." Quickly looking to Joseph, he added, "Don't repeat none of that to yer mother."

The boy covered his mouth and grinned widely behind his hand.

"Can you fix it?" Ordell asked.

"It'll take a bit of time and I might need to visit a black-smith, but I should be able to straighten it out. I can also modify your firing mechanism. I've got those tools in my saddlebag."

"Honest?"

"I should be able to give you a bit more accuracy and I might be able to rig up something to speed up your reloading as well. You think that might put us square?"

Ordell made a show of thinking it over. Reluctantly, he shrugged and turned the meat over the flames. "We'll see."

FIVE

It turned out that Ordell was one hell of a good cook. Even though Clint didn't have a lot of experience with preparing freshly killed bear, he couldn't deny that the meat melted in his mouth like the best steaks he'd ordered in a restaurant.

Afterward, Clint and Ordell had started skinning the bear and then the trapper insisted on finishing up on his own. Rather than argue for more of the dirty work, Clint went back to the fireside and worked on the rifle. Allison and Joseph spent the night telling stories and a few jokes before the boy drifted off to sleep. Clint couldn't keep his eyes open for much longer, himself.

Suddenly, Clint snapped awake and reflexively grabbed for the modified Colt at his hip. The gun was right where it should be, but there wasn't anything in sight for him to shoot. Clint's heart was thumping in his chest and his breathing was ragged. When he closed his eyes, he felt as if he were once again bolting from tree to tree with a rampaging monster at his back.

Although it didn't take long for him to shake himself out of that somewhat dizzy state, Clint found he'd also shaken himself too far awake to go back asleep. He sat up and stretched his arms while pulling in a lungful of air, which still smelled like burning wood.

It was still dark, but the promise of sunrise hung in the eastern sky. There wasn't enough light to see more than a few feet in front of him, but the dampness in the air and the sound of rustling birds made Clint certain that light would break in just over an hour or so.

Since he wasn't about to fall asleep right away, Clint got up and took a quick survey of the camp. That was all he needed to realize that they were missing one person. In particular, they were missing one person with a sweet Georgia accent.

Clint was careful not to wake up Joseph as he stepped over the boy. Judging by the way the kid was snoring, it would have taken another rampaging bear to wake him up. Oddly enough, Ordell slept without making a sound or even stirring a muscle. He sat with his back to a tree, his head slumped forward, and his hands wrapped around a sheathed hunting knife.

At this time of the day, the sound of slowly churning water easily caught his ear. Clint made his way toward that water and pushed aside a thick curtain of hanging branches to find the small lake that they'd all been using for drinking and washing since making camp. Clint hunkered down at the edge of the water and dipped both hands into it. Eventually, he turned to look along the shore of the lake to find Allison sitting there with her arms wrapped around her knees.

"You couldn't sleep, either?" she asked.

"I was doing fine until I ran out of breath. I guess part of me still thinks I'm running."

She smiled and laughed under her breath. "You were kicking your legs. Kind of like an old mutt we had back home."

"That's good to know," Clint said. "You're more than welcome to scratch behind my ears."

This time, she laughed a bit louder. Allison caught herself and quickly covered her mouth before making too much noise. "I don't want to wake up Joseph. He's had a rough couple of days."

"He seems like a strong boy."

"I still worry. It's a mother's job, you know."

"How long have you been sitting here?" Clint asked.

"Maybe an hour. I was just going to get a drink of water, but it's quiet enough for me to hear Joseph from here."

Clint let his eyes wander while focusing solely on his ears. Sure enough, without much effort he could hear the boy's snoring just as plainly as he could hear the early birds chirping among themselves.

"I could also hear you once you started moving around," she added. "I was hoping you'd find your way here."

As she spoke, Allison stood up and walked over to him. She kept her hands in front of her and smoothed out the folds of her skirt right up until she was close enough to speak to Clint in a whisper. "It's only been me and Joseph all the way from Georgia. We've been on trains, stagecoaches, ferries and a few wagons.

"I can protect my son, but I've also had to deal with a lot of men along the way. Most of them look at me like Mark does. I know he probably doesn't mean any harm, but there's something in his eyes that makes me nervous. You, on the other hand . . ." While her words trailed off, Allison reached out with one hand as if to brush something off of Clint's shoulder.

She straightened his collar and let her hand linger a bit so she could feel the skin on his neck. "I like the way you look at me."

"Has it been just you and Joseph for long?"

"Joseph's father was killed just over a year ago. That's why we decided to come all the way to Oregon so we can be by my family. It's taken me this long to raise the money as well as the courage to set off across the country."

"I'll bet it feels good to be this close to the end of your trip."

Slowly taking her hand away from him, Allison sat down close enough to Clint's side that she could keep talking without disturbing the tranquility of the lake. "It does and it doesn't. I'll be glad to give Joseph a solid home again." Grinning, she added, "But part of me will miss all of the adventure."

"Yeah. Going up against a black bear is sort of a tough act to beat."

Slowly, Allison's hand slid across Clint's knee until she gently brushed along his inner thigh. "Actually, I can think of a way to top it."

"Yeah," Clint said as he eased her back so he could roll on top of her. "Something just came to my mind as well."

SIX

The warmth of Allison's body was more than enough to make up for the coldness of the ground beneath them. Early morning dew mixed with a hint of frost to put a chill into the banks of the river. Apparently, she wasn't feeling any of that chill either since she had Clint on top of her to heat her up.

Clint's hands were slowly exploring her body through the layers of her clothing until he could find a way to get beneath it. One of his hands managed to get under her skirts and find the smooth, shapely contour of her leg. The fingertips of his other hand were just beginning to slip under her blouse when he stopped.

"What's the matter?" she asked breathlessly, while midway through opening Clint's pants.

"Should we . . . wait?" he asked against every instinct in his entire body. "At least until we have a little more privacy?"

She smiled and leaned in closer. "You'll just have to be quiet enough for us to hear footsteps if anyone decides to pay us a visit."

"And what about you?"

Giving him a quick grin, she replied, "I don't think I'll have any problem keeping quiet."

"Is that so?"

Taking up the challenge implied in her expression, Clint swept her up in his arms and carried her over to a large tree at the edge of the lake. When he set her down, he could feel one of Allison's legs immediately wrap around him. That way, he was able to slip his hands easily under her skirts and feel the tight curve of her buttocks.

Allison leaned back and let out a breathy sigh. The sound was just loud enough to make her snap her eyes open and glance expectantly in the direction of the camp. When she looked back again, she found Clint smirking victoriously.

"They're still sleeping soundly," she whispered. "Don't get too full of yourself."

Since his pants were already mostly off, Clint took them down the rest of the way and then hiked the front of Allison's skirts up around her waist. The sides and back of her skirts still draped down, wrapping both of them up in soft material.

He could feel the warm dampness between her legs through the thin material of her panties. He could also feel her arms tighten around him expectantly as he pulled her panties aside and entered her.

Allison let out another breath while leaning back. She opened her legs and took all of him inside of her, savoring the way his cock grew harder as he began thrusting in and out. After one particularly strong thrust, the tree shook just enough to scatter the birds that had been in its branches.

With that, Allison got her legs beneath her and pushed Clint back. She smirked at the tortured look on his face and then turned her back to him while sliding her blouse off and dropping it to the ground. She shed every stitch of her clothes in the same fashion, leaving a trail that led right to the edge of the water. By the time she tested the water with one foot, Clint was naked and coming up behind her.

The water was cold at first, but just cold enough to make

every inch of their skin sensitive to the touch. That way, when they found each other in the deeper water, the warmth from their bodies practically melted them together.

Clint once more wrapped his arms around her as they both stood with just their head and shoulders out of the water. One little hop was all it took for her to be wrapped around him. Under the water, Clint barely had to use any strength to keep her up.

Allison's body was strong and muscular, without losing a bit of her femininity. Her arms and legs held on to him tightly and her backside was smooth and firm in his hands. Pert breasts pressed against Clint's chest, with nipples so hard that he could feel them brushing against his skin. While he was savoring the feel of her body against him, Clint felt her hand reach between his legs and guide him once more into her.

This time, the feeling of entering her was like a jolt that ran all the way through his body. Whether it was the coldness of the water, or just the warmth of her skin didn't really matter. All that mattered just then was the two of them alone in that lake as if there were nothing and nobody else in the world.

Allison wriggled slowly as Clint pumped between her legs. He kept his hands on her buttocks so he could move her up and down in time to his own rhythm. She kept pace with him perfectly by grinding her hips back and forth.

As she felt her pleasure building, Allison let go with her arms and allowed her upper body to float back a ways from Clint. All the while, she kept her legs wrapped tightly around him.

Seeing her like that, with her hair spreading around her like a veil and her breasts breaking the surface of the water, made Clint want the moment to last for another couple of hours. Even another couple of days would have been fine.

Suddenly, Allison's eyes snapped open and her face took on an intense, almost desperate expression. She straightened up and wrapped her arms around Clint's neck as her muscles tightened around him. Her breathing was quick and frantic and she whispered urgent moans directly into Clint's ear.

He could feel her orgasm ripple through her much like he could feel the water rippling around him. While she was still trembling against him, Clint felt his own climax rush up onto him and overtake his entire body. For a moment, he thought he might let her go but the cold water kept him alert enough to stay on his feet.

One more pump into her pushed him over the edge and he exploded inside of her. After that, the quiet returned and the first light of dawn came with it.

SEVEN

Clint stepped back into the camp a few minutes after Allison returned. Joseph was just beginning to stir and Ordell was right where he'd been the last time Clint had checked. As if feeling the eyes on him, Ordell lifted his chin and set his eyes on Clint.

"You have a good swim?" Ordell asked.

Clint shrugged and said, "The water's a bit cold, but I got used to it."

Ordell glanced over to Allison and then climbed to his feet. "I bet. You done with my rifle yet?"

"There's a bit more I can do, but I'll need a blacksmith to straighten the barrel properly. My part shouldn't take more than another few hours."

"And there's a blacksmith in Westerlake."

"Westerlake's right on the border of Oregon Territory," Joseph said.

Ordell nodded and patted the boy's head as he walked toward the edge of camp. "You got that right. Since Clint needs a bit more time to fix up my rifle and Westerlake's not even half a day's ride from here, we can have ourselves a leisurely breakfast. Would you mind cooking, ma'am?"

"Not at all," Allison replied cheerily. "I was just going to ask if there's something I could do to help."

"That'd be it, ma'am. I've still got a bit of work to do in skinning that bear."

Joseph's eyes became wide. "Can I watch?"

"Depends on what yer ma says."

Reluctantly, Allison nodded. "I guess it's all right. That is, if Mr. Ordell doesn't mind."

"Just see if you can keep up, boy," Ordell said as he rolled up his sleeves and tramped into the woods.

Joseph practically tripped over himself to run in Ordell's wake.

By this time, Clint had situated himself in the same spot he'd used the previous night. Laying the rifle across his lap, he unrolled a bundle of burlap which held a small sampling of his gunsmithing tools. His hands moved as if they had a will of their own as Clint dismantled a section of the rifle's firing mechanism.

"Do you really know what you're doing with that?" Allison asked.

Clint nodded. "It's my profession to know."

"You're a gunsmith?"

Laughing under his breath, Clint asked, "Why do you find that so hard to believe?"

"I don't know. The way you rode in when we were in trouble and how you handled yourself . . . none of it makes me think you're a gunsmith."

"Well, I suppose I don't fix as many rifles as I used to."

Having uncovered just as much of the bear's carcass as he needed, Ordell hunkered down over the animal and sawed at it with a knife that was almost as big as Joseph's arm. The boy watched from a distance with wide eyes and short breaths.

"Did you kill a lot of bears?" Joseph asked.

Ordell nodded and stripped away another section of the bear's hide. "More'n a few."

"Did you ever get bit by one?"

Glancing over to the boy, Ordell pulled away the collar of his shirt far enough to reveal a patch of skin around his neck that looked more like gnarled leather. "A grizzly got ahold of me right there," he said. "Clamped down so hard that I thought my whole head was gonna come clean off."

"What did you do?"

"The first thing I did? Sounds funny now, but the first thing I did was punch that ol' bear right in the face."

Joseph's head snapped back and then cocked to one side like a confused pup's. "Then what happened?"

"That ol' bear looked right back at me like he didn't know what to think. Then, he sniffed the air, rubbed his nose and said, 'If you wanted me to let go, all you needed to do was ask.'"

For a moment, Joseph scrunched his nose and kept staring blankly at Ordell. Then, a giggle worked its way through him, which nearly doubled the young boy over. When he was able to catch a breath, he said, "That didn't really happen!"

Laughing a bit himself, Ordell cut away the last strip of the bear's hide and started cleaning up all the remaining stubborn bits around the edges. "Maybe not exactly, but that bear did look awfully confused."

"You really punched him?"

"I told you it sounded silly, but a man don't really know what to do in a situation like that the first time it happens."

"So what really happened after that?"

"After that," Ordell said reverently as he raised his bloodied knife and held it up for the boy to see, "I buried this right under his chin and twisted."

Those words tore the smile right off of Joseph's face and left him with the blank, awe-inspired stare that had been there before.

"No man was meant to fight no bear," Ordell said. "Just like no man was meant to outrun no horse. But we got the brains to make guns and trains to do them very things. Some might consider that a way of cheatin' the natural order of things, but it ain't."

Lowering his voice, Ordell said, "When it's down to your life on the line or the life of someone you love, you do whatever you can to be the last one standing. That's the first lesson you need to know growin' up to be a man. If the cards are already stacked against ya, there ain't nothing wrong in doing anything at all to beat 'em."

Joseph blinked and shook his head. "I don't like playing cards."

Ordell blinked as well, but he seemed to be coming out of a trance rather than drifting into one. "Yeah. I guess that's more of a grown-up's game. Come over here."

The boy was reluctant, but quickly worked up enough courage to stand behind Ordell.

After jabbing the blade into the dirt, Ordell reached down and lifted up the bear's huge, limp paw. He then pressed his foot down on top of the paw and retrieved his knife from the ground.

"You see them claws?"

Joseph leaned forward and nodded when he saw the long, curved claws protruding from the bear's paw.

"Indians use them claws like we use knives," Ordell said as he delicately sliced around one of the claws with the tip of his blade. "They also wear 'em around their neck for good luck. It shows the spirits that they went up against the best that nature had to offer and lived to tell the tale."

"Even when the cards were stacked?"

Ordell looked to the boy with genuine surprise. "That's right! Even when they're stacked against ya. And just 'cause you didn't strike the killing blow, that don't mean you didn't buck the odds. If'n anyone says different, just show 'em this."

Joseph was just quick enough to catch what Ordell tossed to him. When he opened his hands, the boy found one of the bear's claws in his grasp. "Can I keep it?"

"That's why I threw it to ya." As he stood up, Ordell pulled the bear's hide from the rest of the dirt that had been covering it and draped it over his shoulders. Even his large frame was stooped under all that dead weight. "Now head back to the camp and tell yer ma to get ready to leave."

EIGHT

The four of them rode in single file along a broken path that led back to the main trail. Clint and Eclipse were at the front of the line. Allison and Joseph shared a horse in the middle, while Ordell brought up the rear. Some more of the wagon had been salvaged to build a sled to carry some supplies, but mostly it had been made to hold the enormous bear skin that was folded over the wooden slats.

Even though dragging that skin slowed them down a bit, the small caravan made it back to the trail before noon. Clint guessed they should catch first sight of Westerlake well before supper. Then again, after all the bear meat he'd eaten, he doubted he'd have much of an appetite.

The first portion of the ride was filled with almost constant chatter from Joseph as he recounted every last detail of Ordell skinning the bear. And when he reached the end of the story, he was more than happy to take a breath and go right back to the start.

"You know what?" Joseph said as he held out the bear claw. "Mr. Adams? You know what Indians say a bear claw will do?"

"Bring him luck?" Clint said, hoping to take just a bit of the wind from Joseph's sails.

"That's right! And you know why?"

Suddenly, Clint pulled back on Eclipse's reins and held up his hand. Although Allison didn't know quite what to make of that gesture, Ordell came up alongside her and brought her to a stop. Looking at the front of the line, he asked, "What do you see, Clint?"

"There's a couple horses coming this way."

"Anyone you know?"

"Can't tell from here, but they're riding just a little too quickly for my liking."

Ordell shielded the sun from his eyes and squinted down the path. He picked out the approaching riders easily and let out a slow, grumbling breath. "Looks like they might be coming from Westerlake."

"Probably."

"And when men like that are riding that fast, it's safe to say they're either after someone or someone's after them."

Clint looked over to Ordell and nodded gravely. "Probably."

"What's the matter?" Allison asked.

Clint dug in his saddlebag and found his spyglass. "Might be nothing," he said. Unfortunately, he couldn't put much faith in those words once he got a look at the faces of those riders. "Still, you might want to head for those trees and wait for them to pass."

Although there were a couple bends in the trail ahead, the riders cut across them to charge directly at Clint and Ordell.

"All right," Allison said. "We'll go and wait."

Clint listened to make sure that she headed far enough away, but he didn't watch her go. Instead, he kept his eyes on the approaching riders. He also patted the side of Eclipse's saddle to make sure that his rifle was where it should be.

"You know these men?" Clint asked.

"I was just about to ask you the same thing. Is my rifle ready to fire?"

"Sure, so long as you don't mind blowing your hands off when the first round gets jammed in the barrel."

Ordell let out a snorting laugh. "Perfect."

"Any reason why they might be so anxious to greet us?"

Shifting in his saddle, Ordell replied, "I guess we'll just have to wait and see."

They didn't have to wait long.

The riders charged straight for them and didn't slow down until they were about to stampede over both Clint and Ordell. As they pulled back on their reins, the riders circled around to close them in. All three of them had dirty faces and several day's stubble on their chins. They also had plenty of guns strapped to their saddles as well as their hips.

Although the men were dressed similarly to Ordell, their eyes were wilder and their faces were much smoother. All three of them were breathing almost as heavily as their horses and did so through slackly hanging jaws.

The rider who'd come to a stop in front of Clint and Ordell was the first to speak. He did so through a mouth that was only slightly marred by a harelip. "Looks like you two've been busy."

"Do I know you men?" Clint asked.

"All you got know is that we're the ones looking to cash in on the reward offered for that bear's skin."

Ordell didn't even blink. Instead, he gazed around as if in a daze and asked, "What bear?"

NINE

Scowling, the first rider grabbed for the pistol that was tucked under the front of his belt. His two partners were quick to arm themselves within the next couple of heartbeats.

"You wanna play dumb with me?" the first rider snarled. "Then it'll be the last mistake you ever make. That bear's worth six hundred dollars, so unhitch it from your damn horse and ride away."

Clint turned slightly to look over at Ordell. "Six hundred dollars? Did you know that?"

"I heard it was eight hundred. This little pecker must be out to pull one over on his friends, here."

"That true?" asked one of the other riders.

"Whatever we get, we'll split," the first rider snapped. "But we don't get nothin' unless we get that skin."

"Why don't you boys go into those woods and find a bear of your own?" Ordell asked in something of an innocent voice. "Or would you rather take yer chances with an old man instead of something like what used to fill that skin behind me?"

"Don't test me, Mark," the first rider snarled. "Or I swear I'll—"

"You'll what?" Ordell barked. "You rode all this way to talk tough? You either jump or get the hell out of our—"

Ordell's words, combined with the vicious tone in his voice, was more than enough to make the first rider bring up his pistol and aim at the older man.

Ordell responded by snatching an old Navy model Colt from under his buckskins and thumb back the hammer.

When he saw the tempers flare up past the boiling point, Clint's first reaction was to check on the riders who'd gotten around behind him. Sure enough, those men were more than ready for a fight and already had their guns up and pointing at Clint's back.

With a quick, backward sweeping motion of his right arm, Clint took his modified Colt from its holster and aimed it at the rider directly behind him. Just as his arm straightened, he pulled the trigger and sent a round into the rider's chest. The lead thumped home and knocked the rider clean out of his saddle.

Before that rider could hit the ground, Clint shifted his aim and fired at the other rider who'd tried to get around behind Ordell. That shot had to be taken from memory and flew wide since that rider had had the sense to move from his previous spot.

Although he was startled at the sudden turn of the tables, the rider behind Ordell pulled his trigger and sent a shot whistling past Ordell's horse's ear. The animal barely seemed to notice and merely shifted from one hoof to another.

Ordell and the first rider were staring each other down, giving Ordell enough time to take aim.

The rider wasn't so anxious to catch any lead, so he fired a quick shot at the older man. His horse had already been fidgeting and this was enough to get it stumbling backward with a few short steps. The movement wasn't enough to shake the rider from his saddle, but it seemed to be enough to throw off his aim. His shot blazed through the air and only clipped a bit of skin from Ordell's chin.

Barely twitching at the sting of the passing round, Ordell hunkered down low and fired a shot at the rider directly in front of him. The younger man buckled and stared wide-eyed at Ordell as he quickly lost the strength to hold up his gun.

The rider behind Ordell had pulled back on his reins to try and put some distance between himself and Clint. He shifted his eyes wildly between his two former targets and waved his gun in front of him.

"Don't do it, kid," Clint shouted. "Just toss the gun and ride away!"

Looking at Clint, the rider seemed to consider taking his advice. Then, his eyes glazed over and steely resolve imposed itself upon his face. With that, he lifted his gun and sighted along the barrel at Clint.

Clint waited for a split second more than he should have before aiming and firing. His shot caught the kid in the forehead and pitched him to the ground faster than if he'd been kicked by a mule.

"Goddamn it," Clint whispered as he saw the kid land in a heap and his horse bolt away from the trail.

Ordell was still looking at the face of the first rider. When Clint turned to see how the older man was faring, he saw a look in Ordell's eyes that was similar to the one that had been there when he was studying the face of the rampaging bear.

The first rider had lowered his gun and used that hand to press against the wound in his chest. He sucked in a breath and wheezed, "You didn't—"

He was cut off by another shot from Ordell's pistol, which bored a hole straight through his heart.

TEN

Clint felt a jolt of panic when he wasn't able to find Allison or Joseph. He'd ridden to the spot where they'd gone and all he saw was a patch of empty woods bordering on even thicker trees. After calling their names one time, he heard them answer back. Only after he saw her horse emerge from those thicker trees did Clint finally take an easier breath.

Since they were already deep in the woods bordering the trail, Clint led them in just a bit deeper before leading them out again.

"The trail's that way," Joseph said as he pointed to his left. "We're not going the right way."

"I know, Joseph," Clint said.

"Was there gunshots?"

"Yes, Joseph. There were."

"How come we're not going back the same way?"

Having no trouble putting the pieces together for herself, Allison patted Joseph's head and said, "This is a short-cut. That's all."

"We're still going into Westerlake?"

"Yes, we are."

"I want to see where the gunfight was."

40

"No, you don't, Joseph," Allison said sternly. "No, you don't."

Clint emerged from the trees a good distance from where the bodies of those riders were lying. Ordell was waiting in that general area, but spotted them quickly and rode to meet them.

Westerlake could be seen after they crested the next big hill. It was a good-sized town with a lumber mill on one edge and a small dock giving boats access to Snake River. Joseph's ears perked up when he heard the lively tolling of a school bell and he began anxiously fidgeting in the saddle.

"Is that where my cousins go to school?" the boy asked.

"I believe so," Allison said. "We'll see it soon enough."

"Why not go see it now?" Clint asked. "We've got business to take care of, but it's nothing Ordell and I can't handle alone."

"Are you sure?"

Clint nodded. "Go on ahead."

"You'll be staying on for a little while, won't you?"

"Sure. If you can recommend a good place for supper, I can meet you there."

"I can do one better," she said. "I can make you a supper better than any restaurant in town."

"Sounds great."

Clint did his best to keep a friendly smile on his face as he got directions from Allison of where she would be. Her family had a house on the river side of town not far from the mill. Even though her instructions were quick and concise, she still had to hurry and spit them out before her son jumped out of his skin.

"I'll be there tonight," Clint said. Leaning down to Joseph, he added, "Try not to scare all those kids with talk about gunfights and bears. Save something for the next day."

"I will, Mr. Adams."

Allison waved over her shoulder as she steered her

horse toward the schoolhouse. Clint watched them leave just long enough to make sure they were on their way. When he looked over his shoulder, he found Ordell waiting there with a pleasant look on his face.

"They're good folks," Ordell said.

Clint nodded and flicked his reins to follow Ordell down the street. "Too bad they had to go through hell and back just to get here."

"Yeah, but it's a tough world. Even staying home don't guarantee you a day's peace."

"Especially when you've got cowboys gunning for you the moment you get within spitting distance of town."

"It looked to me like you had some experience in dealing with that sort of thing."

"And it looked to me like you knew those boys that rode up on us."

Ordell smirked as he swayed back and forth in his saddle. They rode down a street that took them to the end of town that faced the woods rather than the river. Already, the sounds of children had been replaced by the clanging of metal and the grinding of saws.

"I don't spend a whole lot of time in town," Ordell said. "That means this here horse is the best friend I got."

"Then how did that one boy know your name?"

"Did he?"

"I heard him call you Mark, so he either knew you or he took an awfully good guess."

Tapping his heel against his horse's side, Ordell made a clicking sound and got the horse moving a bit quicker. "Come along here, Clint. Let me show you something."

Clint followed Ordell to a long building with a wall that faced the street and was opened by a series of awnings propped up with wooden poles. Skins of all shapes and sizes were piled up under the awnings and the smell of fresh meat hung heavily in the air.

The older man brought his horse to a stop and swung

down from the saddle to land heavily on both feet. His steps were just as heavy as he stomped toward the front of the building and pointed to a notice tacked to the wall.

"You see that?" Ordell asked.

Clint swung down from his own saddle and walked up to the notice. As he did, he could see many of the men working in the building eyeing the sled hitched to the back of Ordell's horse. Soon, those same men were whispering among themselves and pointing at the huge bear skin.

The notice Ordell was pointing at resembled a poster declaring the price put on the head of an outlaw. Instead of a picture of a man, however, there was a drawing of a black bear with a few distinguishing features marked for reference.

Some of those features included things such as a notch chipped from one ear, a discoloration at a spot on its neck and a few cracked teeth. They were characteristics that Clint hadn't even noticed when the bear was alive. After taking a moment to think it over, Clint still had to look back at the bear skin to check if those features were there.

"It's him all right," Ordell said proudly. "But that's not the part I wanted you to see."

Clint then looked at the spot where Ordell's finger was tapping against the wall.

The notice read:

> $800 REWARD FOR SKIN
> OF BLACK BEAR. KILLED
> MEN AND CHILDREN. BRING
> HIDE HERE FOR PAYMENT.

"That there's a lot of money and it's why those boys were after us," Ordell said.

"And that's how those boys knew you?"

"I been a hunter all my life, Clint. I do most of my trading here, so I suppose some of these men know me. You were there. You saw them ride up on us with their guns drawn. By my count, you killed two to my one."

"Yeah, but that doesn't mean I'm happy about it."

"You know what'll make me happy?" Ordell asked with a smirk. "Eight hundred dollars. Let me cash this in and I'll give you your cut."

"Just hand over that rifle," Clint replied. "I passed a blacksmith on the way over here."

ELEVEN

Clint walked into the blacksmith's shop carrying Ordell's rifle. By the time he finally made it into the cramped little shop, Clint actually felt as if he might need to lean against the rifle before he fell over. The gun was heavier than a pickax and twice as difficult to manage.

The blacksmith's shop was the shape of a barn, but about half the size. Outside, there were stray bits of iron and rods of all lengths propped against the wall. Inside, there was a similar mess, but combined with a few anvils and buckets of water scattered in different spots on the floor. In the middle of it all was a stout man with a thick black mustache. He was bald, except for a ring of hair that connected the back of one ear to the back of the other. He wore a dirty shirt with the sleeves torn off and a thick apron stained the same color as the charred floor.

When he saw Clint walk into his shop, the stout man immediately squinted at the rifle he was carrying. "Hey, there. What're you doing carrying Mr. Ordell's gun?"

Clint held the rifle out and blinked in surprise. "You know whose gun this is?"

"Sure I do. I made that barrel."

"Then perhaps you could help me straighten it."

45

The stout man had his hands full with a large pair of tongs and a hammer. He dropped both of those and rushed over to Clint the moment he heard those words. "What'd you do to that gun? Where's Mr. Ordell?" Rather than wait for an answer, he stopped as if he'd been smacked and started shaking his head. "Oh, Lord. This isn't good at all."

"I know," Clint said. "The barrel's bent, but—"

"Bent?! That barrel's nearly twisted in half!"

Clint looked down at it and said, "It's not that bad."

"What's this?" the man asked as he squatted down to get a closer look at the hammer. "This wasn't there before."

"I know. I fixed that up a bit."

"You?"

"The name's Clint Adams. Before you ask, I do know what I'm doing. I'm a gunsmith."

"A gunsmith, huh? I suppose you have some little tools and such to straighten out that iron?"

"No. That's why I came here."

The stout man blinked and straightened up. He used both callused hands to rub his face. When he lowered his hands, he revealed a wide grin and a bit of color in his cheeks. "Sorry about that, mister. I'm just awfully proud of that rifle. It's not often that I get to put together something like that. My name's Aldo."

"You're the one that built this gun?"

"Parts of it, yes. Mr. Ordell designed it, but I had to make the barrel and a good amount of the pieces. It sure was a nice change of pace from all the horseshoes and pots I have to fix."

"I knew these parts were custom-made, but I figured they were put together from parts of other old guns."

"No, sir," Aldo said proudly. "Most of those were made here in my shop. I still got the molds for when Mr. Ordell needs something replaced."

"And how often is that?" Clint asked, knowing that the blacksmith was busting at the seams to answer.

"Never. Not once."

"You wouldn't have another barrel lying around, would you?"

Aldo took the rifle from Clint's hands and looked along it from every angle. "No and I don't need one. Besides, it'd be easier to straighten this one out than to bore out a new one. Mr. Ordell makes his own ammunition, so it takes something extra special to keep them slugs in the air. What happened to this beauty, anyway?"

Clint couldn't help but wince at the thought of what Aldo would say when he heard his pride and joy had been used as a lever. "Just an accident while out hunting. You know how things happen."

"Was it a good hunt?"

"You heard about that bear that's got the price on his head?"

"That black bear that killed them folks?" Aldo asked. "Everyone's heard of that bear."

"Well, it won't be bothering anyone anymore."

Aldo looked down at the rifle in his hands the way a proud parent would look at their baby. "Well, then, I guess I can't be too upset if she's just a little bent. I'll get her straightened out in no time." While making his way toward the small furnace at the back of his shop, Aldo said, "If you've got some time to spare, I wouldn't mind hearing about what you did to this here gun."

At first, Clint tested the waters with a few bits and pieces of the basic things he did to spruce up Ordell's weapon. When he saw the blacksmith responding with genuine interest, Clint slipped right into telling some of the more technical details.

Aldo listened intently as he heated up the rifle's barrel. "That ought to make this here weapon a real work of art. Before you know it, Mr. Ordell's nephew will be coming around trying get one like it for himself."

"His nephew?"

Nodding, Aldo said, "That's right. The boy ain't much of a hunter just yet, but he's eager to learn. He'll be real sore when he hears his uncle got to that bear before he did."

Thinking back to Joseph's eager face, Clint asked, "How old's the boy?"

"Eh . . . I'd say he's damn near twenty. Maybe a little more'n that. I guess that means he ain't exactly a boy no more."

"Twenty, huh? What's he look like?"

Aldo stopped what he was doing to give Clint a puzzled look. "What's he look like? I dunno. Tall kid, dark hair. Clean face."

"Did he have a harelip?"

"Yeah. He did. You know him?"

Clint now thought back to the rider who'd come up to stare down Ordell while demanding rights to that bear skin. "I think I just might."

TWELVE

When Clint walked down the street from the blacksmith's, Ordell was walking along the opposite side and headed straight toward him. Ordell saw Clint almost immediately and put on a wide grin as he approached.

Holding out both hands to pat Clint on the shoulders, Ordell said, "Getting that money was even easier than I thought. Seems the locals that put up that reward were more worried about getting rid of that bear than keeping hold of their cash. How about you buy some whiskey and we can split up the haul?"

Clint kept quiet, since the street was fairly crowded. He bit his tongue all the way to a small shack that was one step away from being out of town. Half of the shack was facing Westerlake, while the other half stretched out into the surrounding woods.

As soon as they got close to the shack's front door, Clint stopped and fixed his eyes on Ordell. The only set of eyes and ears in the vicinity that didn't belong to either man were carried around on four legs. "Who was that kid you shot?"

"You mean the one who jumped us along with those other two? Is that the kid you mean?"

"You know damn well who I mean," Clint said.

Ordell looked around as if he was being ambushed. When he looked at Clint once more, there was a mix of disbelief and humor in his eyes. "I told you before, Clint. That was just a bunch of kids out to get that reward money without having to work for it."

"You sure that wasn't your nephew?" When he asked that question, Clint stared at Ordell the way he would stare at a man from the other side of a poker table. It was a way for him to get a grip on whether someone was lying and it rarely let him down.

This was no exception.

In fact, it worked so well that Ordell knew he wouldn't be able to lie even before he tried to get the words out.

Slowly, the humor on Ordell's face melted away. He nodded slowly and said, "All right. That was my nephew. How'd you know?"

"Your own flesh and blood? Why would you kill—"

"You were there, Clint," Ordell snapped. "I didn't go after that boy. He came after us. With his gun drawn!"

"That's true. And it's a downright shame to be forced to kill someone from your own family under those circumstances. What I don't understand is how you could do that so lightly. You didn't even flinch."

"That kid's always been trouble. You don't know the half of it."

"Then tell me. I've got time to listen."

Clint picked up an unmistakable shiftiness in Ordell's posture and expression as he led the way into the small shack where they'd originally been headed. The older man walked with his shoulders hunched forward and his eyes cast toward the floor. The longer Clint followed him, the more he found himself instinctively allowing his hand to drift toward his holstered pistol.

Inside, the shack was filled with a little bit of everything someone might need if they were on their way to or from the surrounding woods. There were supplies for sale in one corner, food being served in another and a small bar serving liquor in dirty glasses.

Ordell went straight for the bar and ordered two drinks. Apparently, the barkeep knew Ordell well enough that he didn't have to ask what the man wanted when he made his order. With his drinks in hand, Ordell led the way to a small table close to the small stove where food was prepared.

Taking a glass from Ordell, Clint took a cautious sniff of the liquor before drinking it. The stuff was probably some sort of whiskey, but there was some sort of foam around the edges that didn't seem to belong there. Despite his own misgivings about the drink, Clint saw Ordell swig it down without hesitation.

"Don't ask what's in it," Ordell said after wheezing and setting his glass down. "The owner makes it himself and it's damn good."

Clint took a gamble along with a sip from the glass. Despite the fact that he couldn't quite pin down what he was tasting, he had to admit it tasted pretty good. Even so, he set the glass down before diving in again.

"Here's your money," Ordell said as he slapped a stack of bills onto the table.

Thumbing through the stack, Clint took a quick count and looked back up to Ordell. "That's about half the reward."

"You wore that bear down pretty good and had him on his last legs. I figure we should split the money."

Clint shook his head and took his hand off the cash. "I'm fixing up your rifle. That makes us even."

"For God's sake, just take the damn money before someone in here gets it in their head to take it fer themselves."

Clint reached out and took half the stack, leaving the rest as if it no longer existed. Sighing loudly, Ordell snatched up the rest of the money and shoved it under the top few layers of skins he wore.

"I'm a peaceful man, Clint. I may be a hunter, but I ain't no killer. Surely someone like you knows the difference."

"Yeah. I know the difference very well."

"I just bet you do. You took out them other two gun hands without much trouble. That, put together with the fancy gun you carry, tells me what sort of things you must do fer a living. And don't tell me you smith guns to put food in yer belly. I know better'n that."

"I've done plenty that I regret," Clint said. "And I'm not here to pass judgment on anyone else. I just didn't have you figured for someone who would do something like that."

"Things happen and most the time we don't have much of a say about it. You want to know what makes them pass a lot easier?"

"Sure."

Ordell held up his glass, smiled and took a sip. "That boy threatened to kill me more'n once over the years. He decided to try and get rich with this hunt no matter what. I told him before I set out on that bear's trail that if he faced me down one more time, I wouldn't think about the blood flowing through our veins before I spilled his. He pushed it. I did what I had to do. Story's over."

Perhaps it was the convincing way that Ordell spoke, or perhaps it was the strange concoction he was drinking, but Clint felt his blood cool and his anger dwindle. Just thinking about a few of the corners he'd been forced into made Clint much more sympathetic to Ordell's situation. Even so, there was plenty more that even the liquor couldn't wash away.

"All right, then," Clint said. "I wanted an explanation and I got it. Why'd you start off trying to lie? We may not be old friends, but we've saved each other's lives twice in one trip. That usually carries a bit more weight."

"I said it before and I'll say it again," Ordell declared. "Yer a good man and one hell of a fine shooter. Just riding with you and them other two for that short amount of time was enough to give me a notion of how you'd react if you knew that boy was my own kin."

Clint couldn't help but wince at that one. "I can't really fault you for that."

"At least you had the decency to accuse me over a drink."

Raising his glass, Clint said, "Here's to not making the same mistake twice."

"Too late for me on that account," Ordell grumbled. "Way too damn late."

THIRTEEN

Clint was still feeling some of the bite from the drink he'd had when he was walking farther into town a half hour later. Westerlake was filled with as many folks in suits as it was with those who followed Mark Ordell's train of thought where clothing was concerned. The streets were crowded with gamblers, ranchers, mountain men and trappers.

It didn't take much to see why so many would be drawn to the place. As he toured the streets, Clint found traders of all kinds and more than enough shops to tickle anyone's fancy. Even though he felt his own spirits rise due to the crisp breeze coming in from the river, Clint caught more than a few locals turning the other way when he tipped his hat to them.

At first, he figured it was because he was a new face in town. After seeing how many others there were that couldn't be locals, Clint guessed it was something else. Before he could get too suspicious, Clint felt the wind change directions and push a pungent smell right into his face.

Unfortunately, that smell was his own.

Clint walked into the first barbershop he could find and tossed his hat onto one of the hooks on the wall. "I need a shave and a bath," he said.

The barber was a tall man with dark skin and angular features. His clothes appeared to be fresh from the laundry and he spoke with a friendly tone in his voice. "If you get a trim to go with it, you can have the whole thing for two dollars." Looking up from the broom he was pushing, he added, "I'd recommend you take the bath first."

"Sounds good to me," Clint said. "Point me in the right direction."

The barber pointed him out the back door and to an area behind the building that was sectioned off by a series of walls. There were three stalls sectioned off, each of which had its own metal tub, stool and clothes rack. While Clint hung his clothes on the rack, a few pitchers of hot water were brought out to him to take the edge off the buckets of cold water that were already there.

The cold water felt good enough as Clint eased himself into it. As the hot water was poured in, however, Clint found himself sinking in the tub as deep as he could go. As he washed up, the stench that had caught his attention earlier disappeared amid the fragrance of lavender the barber tossed in for free.

"There now," the barber said as Clint walked into the shop while drying behind his ears. "That's a whole lot better."

"It sure is."

"Now, are you ready for that shave and trim I offered?"

"Why not?" Considering how good it felt to get out from under all that dirt, Clint was in anything but a disagreeable mood.

The barber smiled and showed the way to one of two large chairs facing the front door. After Clint eased himself into that chair, he was covered by a starched white sheet and then cranked back into a reclining position.

"Looks like you've been out hunting," the barber said.

Clint chuckled as his hair was snipped by the barber's scissors. "That's a polite way of saying I smelled like a wild animal."

"I always try to be polite."

"Well, you're right. Although I didn't intend on doing much of any hunting."

"Really?" the barber asked. "How's that happen?"

"I saw pieces of freshly busted wood on the trail I was riding and then saw a spot where something big had crashed through the bushes. There was a busted wagon not far off the trail, which also caught the eye of a black bear."

The barber now had a comb in one hand and scissors in the other as he tended to the part on top of Clint's head. "Oh, we've had some troubles with a bear around here recently. There's a reward posted for it."

"I know. Another trapper was closing in on it when the bear came at us. Between the two of us, we managed to take it down."

"Is that so? That's a fine bit of hunting. Who was the other man?"

"Mark Ordell. You know him?"

After a few moments, the barber muttered, "Can't say as I do. I know a Lisa Ordell, though. She's lived here in town for a good while."

"Does she have any children?"

"Actually, yes. Two boys and a daughter."

"Do you know her very well?" Clint asked.

"Oh, just a little. She comes in here for bath salts and such. I am the finest barber in Westerlake."

"I can tell."

"She was awfully worried about her boy, Josh, the last time we talked, though. She was so upset the last time she was in that I meant to check up on her to see how things turned out. I try to keep up on things like that with my customers."

Clint had no doubt about that, since almost as much gossip was tossed around barbershops as it was around saloons. Rather than point out that fact, however, he kept his eyes closed, his hands folded across his belly and his voice casual. "What was she so upset about?" he asked.

"Seems her boy fancies himself as a hunter, much like plenty other young men around here. You ask me, I'd tell you that hunting is a whole lot better than the other sorts of trouble a man can get himself into with a gun. Actually, I believe I did tell her that much."

"Makes sense."

The more the barber talked, the more he seemed to fall into a flow where his hands and mouth worked at an equal pace. All Clint had to do from there was sit back, give the occasional push in the right direction and listen to everything the other man had to say.

"That boy was always into something or other," the barber said. "It wasn't until lately that I heard he'd started running with another couple of boys that were never up to anything good. I think that's when Miss Ordell started worrying he might get himself killed."

"Killed?"

"Oh, yes. The way she talked, she felt like she had something to do with the boy's troubles."

"Mothers are like that."

"Yes, but she mentioned someone else came along that made things awfully hard. Not long after that, I heard Josh put his nose where it wasn't wanted and that he was practically out running for his life."

"Was it trouble with the law?" Clint asked.

Grumbling a bit, the barber brushed some stray pieces of clipped hair from Clint's sheet and shook his head. "I don't think so," he said while stirring up some lather from a mug and then brushing it onto Clint's face. "The sheriff comes here to get his hair cut every other week and he didn't mention it."

"Maybe he just didn't feel like mentioning it."

"No, I asked. He didn't know. Miss Ordell looked awfully troubled and I had to know for sure. Whatever trouble that boy was in, it wasn't with the law. Besides, Miss Ordell was usually so friendly when she came in here. Once Josh got into trouble, she walked under a dark cloud that seemed like more trouble than her boy spending a night or two in jail."

"I'll bet you'd know if he did."

"I probably would," the barber admitted. After putting his mug down and picking up his razor, he added, "And he didn't. Near as I can figure, Josh got caught up in something that was more than he could handle. Lord knows that happens to plenty of young men his age."

Clint had to keep from chuckling as the barber shaved him. "You ever think about becoming a detective?"

"No, sir," the barber replied. "I do just fine with my shop."

"The best in town."

FOURTEEN

After cleaning up, Clint found a place where Eclipse could get brushed and fed before scouting out a good hotel for himself. Clint settled on a place that was closer to the river end of town and was lucky enough to rent the last room overlooking the water. He also got a real good view of the docks used for traders, but wasn't about to complain.

After all that walking around, Clint felt a hunger in his belly that quickly became a rumble in his ears. He changed into some clothes that better suited his freshly cleaned face and then walked down to the little stretch of houses where Allison had told him to be for supper.

As he approached the second house in the row, Clint could smell everything from pies baking to biscuits burning and every last bit of it only made him hungrier. By the time he knocked on the door, he considered begging for scraps in the event he'd gone to the wrong house.

Fortunately, Joseph was the one who pulled open the door.

"Mr. Adams! You came!"

"Of course I came," Clint said. "I'm hungry."

Without missing a beat, the boy turned and shouted over his shoulder, "Momma, Clint's hungry!"

Wincing at how bad that sounded, Clint started explaining himself the moment someone else came to the door. "I was just kidding around with Joseph," he said to a stern-looking old woman with her hair tied up in a bun. "I came to visit, not just eat."

"You don't want any of our food?" the old lady asked.

"No. I meant . . ."

She broke into a smile that was warmer than the heat coming from her own kitchen. "Come on in, Mr. Adams. We were expecting you."

Clint took off his hat and walked into the house. It was fairly small and full of chairs, cases and several bookshelves, but had the comforting feel that only organized clutter could bring. His eyes were immediately drawn to the kitchen, which was actually just the rear section of the three-room home. Allison was there, busily tending to several bubbling pots.

"There you are, Clint! I was wondering if you were ever going to show."

"I didn't want to get here too early," he said.

"That's partially my fault. I was so anxious after all that happened, I had to keep my hands busy. I've been cooking all day."

The old woman made her way to where Joseph was tearing a hunk from a loaf of bread and swatted the boy's hand. "And Joey's been eating all day."

"Have not," the boy grumbled as he tore off his bread and skulked away.

The old woman smiled even wider as she watched the boy leave. Turning to Clint, she said, "My name is Sophia, by the way. I've heard a lot about you."

Clint shook the woman's hand. The strength in her grip was hard to miss. "Obviously not enough to prevent you from letting me into your home."

"Well, I must admit you're cleaner than I would have thought."

"Mother!" Allison said in a surprised shout that made her seem more like a teenaged girl than a mother, herself. "He's a guest."

Sophia shrugged and walked over to the stove. "I've seen plenty of hunters and plenty of trappers. They are hardworking men, but usually they're dirty. That's all."

"Well, thanks to the best barber in town, I'm not so dirty anymore," Clint said.

It wasn't long before the table was set and the food began filling the plates. Clint sat back and watched as a feast was spread out before him that made him hungry enough to start chewing at the table. Thankfully, dinner was started before he had to resort to such drastic measures.

The night was full of small talk and bad jokes, which went on all the way through dessert. Once he'd had his fill, Joseph darted from the table and shot outside. Sophia insisted on cleaning up, leaving Clint and Allison by themselves. Judging by the sly grin on Sophia's face, that arrangement was no accident.

"The river isn't far from here," Sophia said. "Just a short walk. You two could use the fresh air."

"Would you like to take a walk?" Allison asked.

Clint grinned at the way the daughter allowed herself to be not-so-subtly guided by her mother. "Sounds like the perfect end to a perfect dinner."

As the door shut behind Clint and Allison, Sophia smiled with the satisfaction of a job well done.

FIFTEEN

The sun was just high enough to cast a golden glow on the water as Clint and Allison walked along the lake. It was early enough in the season for the summery warmth to be wiped away almost as soon as the sun started going down. Still, it was late enough for the night to be comforting rather than cold.

"I thought Mark would have come with you," she said.

Clint shook his head. "The last I saw of him, he was walking back into the woods."

"Walking? Does that mean he'll be back soon?"

"I doubt it."

She wrapped her arms around herself and leaned in a little closer to Clint. As soon as she felt his arm drape over her shoulders, she melted against him even more. "That's too bad. I would have liked to see him one more time. Did he sell that bear skin?"

"He sure did. In fact, I'd bet that everyone in town will be seeing plenty of that carcass as soon as those men get it nailed to the side of their store. Things like that can keep a place in business."

"Are you serious?"

"Of course," Clint said. "How often do you get to look at the hide of a famous bear?"

Clint managed to keep a straight face for a solid thirty seconds. When he started laughing at himself, Allison was quick to join in.

"I'm just glad it's over," she said.

The silence that followed those words was enough to catch her attention. When she looked at Clint, that silence only grew thicker.

"Aren't you glad it's over?" she asked.

"I just hope it is."

"What do you mean?"

Snapping himself out of his thoughts, Clint held her tighter and said, "Nothing. Sorry about that."

"You never got a chance to tell me what happened with those men that met up with you and Mark outside of town. I'd like to hear about it."

"It wasn't much."

"I might have been away from you all," she pointed out, "but I could still hear the gunshots, Clint. I know it was something." She turned around without breaking his grasp. That way, her body was pressed against him while she looked up directly into his eyes. "You stood between us and those armed men. There's nothing to be ashamed of about that."

Clint told her about what happened, leaving out the messier details. He recounted the fight more like a newspaper story than something that actually happened not too long ago. When he was finished, Clint could feel Allison's heart beating powerfully against him.

"My God," she whispered. "You could have been killed. I mean, you hear people say that sometimes, but you . . . really . . . could have died. Thank you."

Her words were genuine. That much was obvious. Yet, somehow, they still didn't ease Clint's nerves. When she finally eased up on her hug, Allison found Clint gazing up at the stars as more and more of them showed up overhead.

"That wasn't the first time Ordell was in a gunfight," Clint said.

"How do you know?"

"Mostly a hunch. Part of it's how he handled himself. I've seen the way people act when they're under fire and it's a rare man who can keep his nerve."

"He's a hunter," she pointed out. "He lives by his gun. My father used to hunt a lot and he barely even flinched when they went off."

"It's different when someone's pointing a gun at you and threatening to pull the trigger. Even if a man can keep his nerve with a gun in his face, there's even fewer who can actually hold up once the lead starts to fly. One thing's for certain, though. Animals are a lot steadier than men."

Allison shook her head as if a fly had buzzed into her ear. "Did you say . . . animals?"

Clint nodded. "Something's been nagging at me and I think part of it was the way Ordell's horse reacted during that fight. It didn't even twitch."

Since she didn't seem to know what else to say to that, she asked, "Did yours?"

"No. That's my point. My horse is like most others. It'll get used to the sound of gunshots after enough of them are fired over its head. They have to train horses in the army so they don't rear up or bolt once things get bad. That's not the sort of thing you find in a trapper's horse."

"Maybe he bought it from an old cavalry officer," she offered.

Clint let that settle for a moment before he said, "The man he killed wasn't much more than a boy. Wasn't even twenty yet."

"Doesn't take twenty years to make a killer."

"He was Ordell's nephew."

Allison didn't have an answer for that one. Instead, she

took a breath and let her eyes wander toward the same stars that had caught Clint's attention.

"I don't know why that still bothers me so much," Clint said. "There's been plenty of times a man's been forced to shoot his own brother. Hell, that happened plenty of times during the war."

"It sounds to me like it's not just that one thing that bothers you, Clint. Maybe it's all of these things that don't sit right."

"Maybe. Or maybe I've just been around too long and seen too many things to let anything go."

"If anything bothers you too much, that just means you need to set it right."

"There's not much left for me to do."

"If Mark's nephew lived here in town, then maybe the rest of his family did."

"The boy lived with his mother," Clint said.

"Does she even know he's dead?"

"That's a good question," Clint said as he thought about what he'd heard from Ordell as well as all the things he'd heard from that nosy barber. "There might be a few things to see to around here after all."

SIXTEEN

Although Westerlake was a fairly large town, all Clint needed to do was pay another visit to Aldo and ask the barber where Miss Ordell lived. He said he needed to see her to pay her respects and that was exactly what he intended to do. Since the excitement of seeing that bear skin on display had spread through the town, the barber wasn't exactly surprised that Clint wanted to check in on the sister of the man who'd put it there.

It was an hour before noon and the day was already turning out to be a hot one. Clint made his way to a row of narrow, two-floor houses situated on the half of Westerlake closest to the woods. He had to knock on the door twice before anyone came to answer it.

Eventually, the door opened a crack and a timid eye looked outside. "My brother's not here," came a tense little voice.

"My name's Clint Adams. Perhaps your brother mentioned me?"

"I didn't see him."

It didn't take finely honed instincts to pick up on the tension in her voice when she mentioned her brother. Clint did his best to put on a friendly smile and make his voice as close a match to that smile as possible.

"Actually, ma'am, I'd like to talk to you."

"Me?" the voice asked.

"Are you Josh Ordell's mother?"

He could see movement through the crack, which might have been a nod on the other side. Suddenly realizing that she wasn't exactly easy to see, she opened the door a bit more and said, "If Josh is in trouble, take it up with the law. I don't want no part of it anymore."

Shifting on his feet, Clint asked, "Would it be all right if I came inside?"

She thought it over and then started to open the door. When she caught sight of the Colt on Clint's hip, she pushed the door closed until the opening was just a crack again. "Who are you?"

"I met up with Mark Ordell a few days ago. We both took on that bear."

"Sure you did, mister."

"I also fixed his rifle. It looks like an old musket with a carving on the stock. His initials were engraved on the trigger."

When she heard that last part, the woman allowed the door to open again. "They're my father's initials. Well . . . our father's."

"That's an odd spot for an engraving."

"When Daddy gave Mark his first rifle, he had his initials carved onto the trigger. He said that way Mark might just remember the lessons he was taught before he goes out and blows his own damn head off by mistake."

Clint nodded. "Seems like he learned a lot. That's a hell of a rifle to give to a boy."

The woman opened the door all the way and stepped aside so Clint could come in. "He gave Mark an old Winchester, but Mark kept that trigger and put it on every gun

he's had since then." Once Clint was inside, she shut the
door and quickly threw the latch into place. "So you and
Mark really killed that bear?"

"He landed the killing blow, but I had it chase me
enough to get it good and tired."

For the first time since he'd laid eyes on her, Clint saw
the woman smile. Unfortunately, even that wasn't enough
to make her too attractive. She was a small woman with a
slight build. Her hair wasn't dirty, but still looked stringy
and hung straight down over a good portion of her narrow
face.

She might have been a bit taller than she looked, but
carried herself with her shoulders stooped and her chin
hanging low. The smile came and went in a few seconds,
leaving a sad frown in its place. The harsh truth of the matter was that she looked much more comfortable wearing
that frown.

"I don't believe I caught your name," Clint said.

"It's Lisa Ordell."

Clint offered his hand by way of a formal greeting, but
Lisa looked at it like she'd never seen one before. Without
making a production out of it, Clint took his hand back and
stepped into the house.

Compared to the house where he'd had dinner the night
before, this place was more like a cave. All the curtains
were drawn and what little light there was came in thin
beams through cracks in the material or walls, themselves.
Everything from books to clothes to papers and old crates
were piled up in every corner. A few dogs sniffed around
Clint's feet, but they quickly scurried off to get lost somewhere else inside the house.

"People been talking about that bear like it was some
kind of monster," Lisa said. "Mark's been hunting worse
than that since he was a kid."

"And you don't talk to him very much?"

She shook her head.

"Why not?" Clint asked.

"It's a family matter."

After giving up on trying to find a clean place to stand, Clint nudged some things aside with his boot and stood next to the shelf where Lisa rearranged a bunch of glass statues. "Actually, I thought I should come by to talk to you. It's about your son."

Hearing that caused her eyes to brighten and her entire body to perk up. "You've seen Josh? Where is he? Do you know him?"

"I didn't know him, ma'am, but I did see him not too long ago."

"Where was he?"

"He came out to have a word with your brother. There were other boys with him and they were all carrying guns."

As Clint spoke, he could see tears forming in Lisa's eyes. There was also an anger welling up in her that seemed to be pushing those tears out even more. "Who were those boys? Where are they?"

Clint reached out and placed his hands on her shoulders. "Ma'am, your son is dead. I'm so sorry."

Lisa's tears stopped. She let out a breath and shrugged Clint's hands off of her. To his surprise, she didn't need any help standing up. In fact, she seemed to be standing even straighter now than when she'd answered the door.

"That son of a bitch," she whispered. "Mark killed him, didn't he?"

"It was a bad situation and—"

"He killed Josh!" she snarled while glaring angrily into Clint's eyes. "Didn't he?"

Seeing that there was no way for him to make things any better, Clint merely nodded. "Yes, ma'am."

"I want to see him."

"What?"

"My son. I want to see his face. Can you take me to him?"

"I suppose," Clint replied. "But that might not be such a good idea."

"Then why'd you come here, mister?"

Although he was a bit surprised by her brutal frankness, Clint couldn't exactly argue with her reasoning. "I came to find out what happened between your brother and your son. It seemed to me like there was more to it than just two men butting heads."

"There was," she said, confirming Clint's suspicion as well as the story told by a certain barber. "Plenty more. I can tell you what happened after I see my boy. Otherwise, it ain't nobody's business but his."

Clint nodded. "All right. Give me some time to collect my horse and I'll take you to him."

SEVENTEEN

It was a few hours before Clint made it back to Lisa Ordell's house. When he rode up and reined Eclipse to a stop, the Darley Arabian was still breathing heavily from his run. Clint did his best to fix up his rumpled clothes and patted some of the dirt from himself before knocking on the door.

When Lisa answered, she muttered, "Took you long enough," just loudly enough for Clint to hear.

"Sorry about that," he said. "There were some matters that needed to be straightened out. If you'd like, we can go to see your son now."

The door opened a bit more, allowing her to peek outside. Since the sun was blazing down in all its fury, the inside of her house seemed to be all the more darker. She squinted out like a mole peeking from its den and then took a few steps outside.

"We'd best hurry," she said.

Clint climbed back into the saddle and reached down for Lisa's hand. She took it and pulled herself up until she was sitting as comfortably as possible behind him. She wrapped her arms around his middle and hung on as if she were grabbing onto a tree trunk in high wind.

71

Snapping the reins, Clint steered Eclipse back toward the street and into the growing number of others in carts or on horseback. The town was busy as always, but the street seemed to have gotten a bit more crowded since Clint had arrived.

"You'd better hurry," Lisa said.

Rather than ask any questions, Clint gave the reins another flick. Despite his size, Eclipse had no trouble at all navigating between the slower animals and vehicles in his way. The stallion wove between them like he was threading a needle until finally he broke into a clearer stretch of road.

Clint headed for the edge of town, noticing that he could still hear plenty of other horses even though there weren't many in front of him. Taking a quick look over his shoulder, he spotted two riders directly behind him. They were both the same age as the riders he and Ordell had encountered outside of town.

"Those boys look familiar to you?" Clint asked.

Lisa twisted around in the saddle and then righted herself. "Yes. That's why I told you to hurry."

"Who are they?"

"Josh knows them."

"And you don't?"

Although she didn't answer right away, Clint could feel the tension in Lisa's arms as she grabbed on tighter to him. He could also feel her head bump against his back as if she were hanging it in shame.

Finally, she said, "They been threatening me to get to my brother. Lately, they been trying to get ahold of Josh as well."

"What do they want?"

Before she could respond, one of the men behind Eclipse let out a piercing whistle. "It's her all right!" he shouted. "Looks like the bitch hired some protection to get her out of town!"

"To hell with that," another of the riders said.

The moment he heard the horses close in on him, Clint snapped the reins and touched his heels to Eclipse's side. "Hold on tight," he said.

Lisa did just that and pressed her face against Clint's shoulder.

They might have been in a less crowded section of town, but Clint still didn't want to start any trouble there if he could help it. There were already too many things that didn't sit well with him and Clint didn't want to add accidentally harming a local to the mix.

Although they'd been headed toward the only end of town that didn't face onto the river or the woods, Clint steered Eclipse toward the wooded half and bolted through a crossroad just as two wagons were about to pass each other. He could hear those other riders getting tangled up with the wagons and took that opportunity to steer down another road.

"How many of these men should I expect?" Clint asked.

"I don't know," Lisa replied. "I've been locked inside my house with the windows shut so I wouldn't have to think about them."

"Well, it looks like we might have shaken them loose."

"And what if we didn't?"

"In that case," Clint said as he left most of the town behind him and snapped Eclipse's reins, "we'll just have to make them regret getting on their horses today."

Clint couldn't tell if he felt relief or fear coming from the mousy woman behind him. Whichever it was, it made Lisa hold onto Clint that much tighter.

EIGHTEEN

Judging by how fiercely the other riders bolted through the more crowded section of town, they weren't about to let Clint get away from them. Even though Clint had every confidence that Eclipse could outrun any of those other horses, he decided to slow down and let them catch up once they were on the outermost edge of Westerlake.

The trail still had a few buildings along its edges, but most of them were about to fall over. Since they were pretty much abandoned as well, Clint slowed Eclipse down and circled around one of the bigger buildings. The place felt like an abandoned boomtown, which was odd since the sounds of the more populated area could still be heard.

"Why are we stopping?" Lisa asked as she nervously tapped Eclipse with her heels.

Eclipse waggled his head and let out a few annoyed snuffs, but didn't move a muscle in response to Lisa's kicking.

"Just climb down here and stay put."

Looking around at the empty lot behind the building, Lisa shook her head. "I'll be fine with you."

"Just do as I say. You either trust me or you don't and if you don't trust me, you're better off on your own."

74

Unable to come up with a good argument, Lisa grudgingly slid down from Eclipse's back. Clint took hold of her arm to help her down, but Lisa quickly pulled away from him. "You'd better come back for me," she said.

But Clint was already riding back around the building to leave her alone. Lisa leaned against a wall, crossed her arms and closed her eyes so she could focus more on listening to what happened in the street.

Clint just made it back around the building when he spotted the other riders charge straight toward him. There were four of them this time and they came to a skidding stop the moment they caught sight of Clint.

One of the riders was older than all of the riders that had met Clint and Ordell outside of town. In fact, he looked like one of the mountain men that had been at the trading post where the bear skin was now on display. His face was covered by a bushy beard and he wore a pistol strapped across his belly.

Two of the riders were Indians dressed in dusty jeans and faded shirts. One of those Indians had a shotgun in hand, while the other kept his rifle in the holster on the side of his saddle.

The fourth rider was closer to the others Clint had seen before. He was a clean-shaven kid with long, stringy hair. He was also the first one to jump down from his horse and stomp forward as if he meant to pull Clint down to his level.

"Get back here, Will," the mountain man said, "before you get yourself hurt."

Will stopped where he was, but didn't take one step back. "Where is she?" he asked Clint. "We know you had her. What'd she do? Hire you to get her past us?"

"Why would she need to do that?" Clint asked.

"You could ask her bastard kid about that."

Clint's eyes narrowed as he studied the faces around him. As near as he could figure, none of those men knew Josh was already dead.

"Just take a step back, kid," Clint said. Looking over to the mountain man, he asked, "What the hell's the meaning of this?"

"I know you was with Mark Ordell. I saw you and him splitting up that reward money."

"So?"

"So tell me where he is or we'll just start shooting pieces off of you until you feel like talking."

With that, the mountain man and both Indians got their weapons ready to fire. None of them took aim, but that didn't make Clint feel any better.

"What's your problem with Mark Ordell?" Clint asked.

The mountain man's lip curled under his beard as he stared unblinkingly at Clint. He spoke in a gravelly rasp when he asked, "You really don't know, do you?"

"If I did, why would I ask?"

"Then what are you doing with that woman?"

Deciding to test the waters a bit more, Clint replied, "None of your business."

"What about the men that bastard killed?" the mountain man snarled. "Is it their business?"

"You know something? I'm getting pretty damn sick of hearing you talk about things that I've never even heard about before. If you're so pissed off at me, then at least tell me why. If it doesn't have to do with me, then ride away and we can all get back to our lives."

"Watch your tongue, mister," Will said. "You'll tell us where that bitch is and you'll do it real quick."

Clint couldn't help but notice that Will's hand had tightened around his gun. The kid had holstered the weapon when climbing down from his horse, but now held onto the grip as if he were about to clear leather at any second.

"Or what, boy?" Clint snarled.

The fierceness in Clint's eyes was almost enough to back the kid all the way to his horse. Although Will didn't quite move that far away, he did take a couple steps back before he managed to push down the instinct.

"Damn it, Will, get back here," the mountain man snarled.

But the kid wasn't listening. His eyes were narrowed down to slits and his lips were drawn tightly against his teeth.

Clint realized he was gritting his teeth almost as much as the kid. Since he had enough experience to know where bad intentions could take two armed men, he let out a breath and slowly held his hands to the sides to show Will his empty palms.

"It's been a long couple of days, kid," Clint said. "Let's not make it any worse."

Will shook his head.

Leaning forward in his saddle, the mountain man barked, "I said get back here right now!"

Still shaking his head, Will planted his feet. "To hell with that," he said. Then, he pulled his gun from its holster and even managed to touch his trigger before a shot from Clint's modified Colt punched through his chest.

NINETEEN

There was an instinct in Clint's head that wanted him to shift his aim and fire at the other gunmen before they opened up on him. But he managed to push that instinct down since he didn't see one bit of movement from any of those three other men. Still, he kept the Colt in his hand just to be safe.

Smoke curled from his barrel as Clint let his eyes sweep over the remaining gunmen.

Moving just his mouth, the mountain man said, "Crow, pick him up."

The Indian with the rifle kept his eyes on Clint while climbing off his horse. He landed on the balls of his feet without making more than a subtle crunch of dirt. Still keeping his rifle at the ready, he walked over to where Will had landed and easily hefted the kid over one shoulder.

As Crow strapped the body to the kid's horse, the mountain man said, "That wasn't supposed to happen, mister. You gotta believe me on that."

"Why should I?" Clint asked.

"No reason, except that me and these two Indians could have gunned you down where you stand if we wanted to."

Clint nodded slowly. "Maybe. Why'd this kid want to get his hands on that lady so badly?"

"Because she's the only one that Josh would have spoken to. And she's also the only one around here who knows what her brother's been doing these last few years."

"Mark?"

"That's the one."

"What's he been doing?" Clint asked.

"Making a hell of a living scalping Crow and Three's people for one."

When Clint looked over to the Indians, he saw their faces darken as if ghosts had just drifted past them.

"He's also been putting together hunts for himself and a few rich folks," the mountain man continued. "And he ain't been hunting much of anything on four legs."

"He hunts people?"

The mountain man nodded. "Been doing it for a while. His nephew found out about it and tried to do something about it. He got a little squeamish, though, when push came to shove and he decided not to take what he knew to the law like he said he would before. That's when me and some of the other relatives of folks that were killed got together to do some convincing of our own."

Clint scowled and shook his head in disgust. "And that includes convincing women like Lisa Ordell?"

"Your friend Mark Ordell don't just kill men. He's killed women and children in order to flush out his prey. One poor lady lost her leg in a trap and Mark was the one who kept her out there screaming until the right person heard her. I've got plenty more of these stories, but the longer I sit here talking to you about them, the more of a head start Mark gets."

"So why waste your time here?"

"Because we want the woman," the mountain man replied. "I doubt Mark has enough of a soul left to care if we hold her hostage, but there's always that possibility. Even if he don't care, she's got to know something about where he went or what he's got in mind."

"I'm not letting you take her," Clint said plainly. "Whatever Mark's done, hurting her won't help matters. It'll just make you every bit as bad as he is."

The mountain man shook his head slowly. "After I lost my own kin to that killer, I have a real hard time caring about what's right or wrong anymore. All I know is that Mark Ordell needs to die and he needs to die real slow.

"The only reason I'm not saying the same about you is because I'm startin' to think you truly didn't know who you were working with. You can prove me right by putting this place behind you and letting us do our work, because it's gonna get real bloody before too long and you'll do well to stay clear of it."

"Mourn your dead and honor their memory," Clint said. "But don't spill more blood in their name."

"This ain't for them," the mountain man said. "You can be damn sure about that."

TWENTY

Clint rode around the building and had no trouble whatsoever finding Lisa. That was due to the fact that she was
standing right where he'd left her, with her arms crossed
and a bored look on her face. For a second, Clint considered asking if she'd even heard the gunshots.

"Where'd those men go?" she asked.

"Away," Clint replied while reaching a hand down to
her. "Now let's do the same."

"You sure they're gone? Those bastards've been coming
after me relentless. Especially that kid."

"The kid's dead. Now, let's get moving."

Oddly enough, Lisa seemed a bit shocked by the blunt-
ness in Clint's voice. She took his hand, climbed onto the
saddle behind him and held on for the ride. Her grip relaxed a bit when Eclipse rounded the corner and she could
see that the rest of the street was as empty as Clint had
claimed.

They rode in silence all the way out to the spot where
Clint and Ordell had met up with Josh and the other riders.
Clouds had rolled in from the north to cast a gray hue to
the sky, while also adding the cold promise of rain. That
seemed to be enough to keep the road clear, since they

81

didn't pass a single other soul until they got into the trees where Clint had told Allison to go and hide.

Lisa kept her face resting against Clint's shoulder until she felt the Darley Arabian come to a stop. She then looked around as if she'd just woken up from a sleep.

"This the place?" she asked.

Clint pointed toward a mound of freshly turned dirt that was marked by a simple cross made from two lashed-together boards. It was a simple grave, but it was the best Clint could manage when he'd raced out to this spot earlier to bury the kid rather than have his mother see him lying where he'd been dropped.

Lisa climbed down and walked slowly toward the grave. She stood there for a few seconds, gazing at the cross. Then, she muttered, "I want to see him."

"He's there, Lisa," Clint said. "Trust me."

Shaking her head, she lowered herself to her knees with her hands folded in her lap. "It ain't about trust. I just . . . need to see his face. I need to see my boy's face."

Any other time, the request might have seemed odd. The solution to the request would have definitely seemed morbid, but the sorrow in Lisa's voice told Clint everything he needed to know.

Getting to his knees, Clint brushed away some of the dirt closer to where the cross was planted in the ground. "He's right here," he said.

Lisa's hands moved in to push away the dirt while brushing Clint away in the process. Her eyes were focused upon the ground and stayed that way until her hands finally touched something that wasn't the ground itself.

Letting out a trembling breath, she dug a little more and then finally uncovered the kid's face. Lisa uncovered Josh's shoulders and part of his chest before she lost the energy to move. Her hands stayed buried in the dirt and were the only things keeping the rest of her body propped up.

Clint couldn't make out what she whispered and didn't

even try. Whatever they were, those words obviously weren't intended for his ears. He took a few steps back and waited until she straightened up, collected herself and started pushing the dirt back onto her son.

"Mark killed him?" she asked.

"Yes, ma'am. Josh had a gun drawn and looked ready to pull the trigger himself, but Mark did kill him."

"So, maybe he had to and maybe he didn't. I guess I'll never know."

"You don't seem too surprised by all of this."

She shook her head slowly. "It's been brewing for a good, long while."

"If you tell me what happened, there's a chance I could do something about it."

Lisa Ordell looked at Clint as if she were staring all the way down to his soul. Her mouth was closed tightly and her hands were clasped in front of her so hard that her knuckles had gone white. "And just what could you do about it? You intend on bringing my boy back to me? You're too late for that. You intend on dragging my brother back here? I don't ever want to see that man's face again."

"Why would Mark kill his nephew?" Clint asked.

Only now did Lisa look away from Clint's face. She seemed to have seen what she needed to see, which made her talk in a solid, unwavering tone. "Mark's been hunting things since he was a boy. My father hunted and even I hunted. But Mark started becoming something else. He became a killer and I don't know why.

"What I do know is that Mark started getting into fights just so he could fight. He got himself into bad spots so he wouldn't have any choice but to shoot his way out of it. At some point he stopped looking for excuses and he began to just kill for the sake of the kill."

Glancing down at the cross, she said, "Somehow, Josh found out about it. My boy loved his uncle and followed him around whenever he was in town. One day he saw

Mark chase down a man and run him through the woods like a deer. This is what he told me."

"Go on," Clint said.

"Josh went to him and found out that Mark had done this plenty of times. It took a while, but Josh finally came and told me about it when he heard that one man Mark killed didn't do nothing to nobody." Blinking and looking at Clint, she added, "Josh used to see them notices at the sheriff's office about wanted men. He used to ask me if his uncle Mark ever caught one of them, so I guess Mark might have mentioned being a bounty hunter somewhere along the way.

"But Ed Gray never harmed a hair on a dog's head, much less did anything to warrant being killed the way he was."

"Ed Gray?"

She nodded. "He was found gutted in the woods a year ago. Gutted," she repeated. "Like an animal. Just the way Mark used to gut the animals he and our father used to kill." Lisa shook her head as more tears streamed down her face. "I didn't know what to do. Josh wanted to confront Mark about it, but I told him not to because I knew Mark would hurt him. I just knew.

"Josh must have told someone else about it, because folks started coming to me and demanding I tell them what I'm telling you now. Right about then, Josh lost track of Mark. When that reward was posted for that bear, we both knew Mark would go after it. That's just the sort of thing Mark lives for.

"Josh got it in his head to find Mark by following that bear and then giving the reward money to Ed Gray's family or anyone else he could find that Mark had hurt. It sounds silly," Lisa said in disbelief. "And I told him as much."

"It's not silly," Clint told her. "It sounds like the best solution he could come up with at the time. Anyone who would truly do something like that has their heart in the right place."

"Thanks for saying so, but it don't make me feel any better. Mark killed my son and he's still out there doing whatever he pleases."

"Tell me where to find him," Clint said. "And I'll see about getting this resolved once and for all."

She stared at him and nodded. "I believe you'd really do that. If you want to look for him, try my father's old hunting cabin. Mark loved that place and always thought he was the only one that knew about it. Josh also told me of a few spots where Mark was supposed to have taken some of the men that were . . . that were killed."

"I'll find him."

"Do what you want. Right now, I want to be alone with my boy."

Clint gave her some time to mourn in peace.

TWENTY-ONE

Now that he had some names to go along with the accusations, Clint knew he could dig up plenty more regarding the wild things he'd heard about Mark Ordell. Even as he'd waited in the woods for Lisa to walk out to him, he had a hard time imagining those things were true.

Part of that was because Ordell didn't quite seem like the sort to do those things. On the other hand, Clint already had a suspicion that there was plenty running beneath the man's surface.

The part that got under Clint's skin the most was how he could spend time riding alongside a killer without knowing it. After priding himself for so long regarding how well he could sum up another person, Clint felt the sting of being tricked extra hard.

Going along with that was the fact that he'd had his own suspicions the entire time. If he'd done something about it sooner, perhaps things could have gone differently. Finally, he decided to cut himself some slack and admit there wasn't anything he could have done that would have made a damn bit of difference.

At the time, he had no reason to step in on Josh's behalf.

Whoever those other men were that rode with Josh, they meant to shoot Clint and there was no other way around it.

Mark Ordell had, albeit unintentionally, saved Clint's life along with the lives of Allison and her son. Clint needed to remind himself of that just to ease the guilt, which panged at the bottom of his stomach like a hot fist punching him again and again.

The more he looked back on it, the more Clint realized he would have done the same thing and the same people would still have wound up dead. That was the part that stuck under his skin most of all.

After taking Lisa Ordell back to her house, Clint went to the first saloon he could find that was within walking distance of his hotel. He stood at that bar and thought about ordering a whiskey just to make it easier for him to get some sleep.

But by the time the barkeep asked what he wanted, Clint requested a beer. The rage was subsiding and the churning in his gut was going away thanks to the decision he'd made to get to the bottom of all the bloody stories he'd been hearing by finding Mark Ordell.

There were also those other men who'd ridden away to raise whatever hell they liked after allowing Lisa Ordell to get by them. Clint knew damn well there was plenty that they weren't telling him.

"Here's your beer," the barkeep said as he set the mug down in front of Clint.

"Thanks," Clint said. "By the way. Have you ever heard the name Ed Gray?"

Reflexively, the barkeep pulled in a quick breath and winced. "You heard about what happened to Ed? I guess a story like that would tend to travel a ways."

"What's your version?"

"I didn't know him very well, but he seemed like a good enough sort. He came in here every now and then to uh . . .

indulge." When he said that last part, the barkeep nodded toward the other end of the room.

Clint looked over there and immediately picked out a set of three girls clad in low-cut dresses who were more than willing to give him a better glance once they saw him look their way. After waving to the working girls, Clint turned back around toward the barkeep.

"Someone found Ed in the woods," the barkeep said. "Cut open from top to bottom. Damn Injuns. There was a price put on their scalps by the law, but that came only after some locals threatened to take things in their own hands."

"Who paid the bounty?"

"Same locals. It's always easier to fork out some money than to get your own hands dirty."

"I suppose so." Clint took a drink of his beer and asked, "Who collected the reward?"

"Same fellow that collected on that bear skin hanging down the street."

After everything else, Clint wasn't too surprised to hear that.

As a group of loud mill workers stomped into the place, the barkeep excused himself and tended to the fresh batch of customers.

The beer helped calm Clint's nerves and the one after it helped him get some sleep. Before he went to bed that night, Clint had his things packed and ready to go for an early morning ride.

Clint was up before the sun rose the next day. He saddled up Eclipse and rode into the woods as the sky was just shifting from purple to blue. The air was crisp and still damp from the night before, which got Clint's blood racing through his veins.

It took a while before Clint was able to enjoy the weather. In fact, he took the first few hours of his ride to sort through everything that had happened so he could try and make some sense of it all. One thing was perfectly clear: it was all one hell of a mess.

The only thing he could be certain about was that he'd be glad when it was all straightened out.

The trees closed in quickly on either side of the trail. Before too long at all, Clint was hard-pressed to recall that there was a town anywhere in the vicinity. All that lumber rising up around him felt like a wall and the branches stretched out over his head were thicker than most roofs. He was no stranger to the woods, but he already knew that Mark Ordell was perfectly at home in them.

Thinking back to how the older man had moved when he was after that bear, Clint barely recalled Ordell making a sound. In fact, he'd seemed out of his element when he had paved road or wooden slats under his feet. The woods were most definitely Ordell's home.

If half the things Clint had heard about Ordell were true, he wasn't exactly a man to take trespassing lightly.

Clint snapped the reins and rode on.

TWENTY-TWO

The days wore on and Clint only covered a fraction of the miles he would have covered if he had simply been trying to get from one spot to another. First of all, he was moving through a section of woods that only got thicker as he drew closer to the border of Oregon Territory. Nearly half the time, he was forced to walk and lead Eclipse by the reins due to thick tangles of branches that hung down to within a foot or two of his head.

Secondly, he wasn't just trying to get from one spot to another. He wanted to get to the cabin that Lisa Ordell had described before her brother Mark got there. Clint had no way of knowing for certain that Mark was headed in that direction, but it was the best lead he had. Actually, it was the only lead since Mark Ordell had vanished after putting Westerlake behind him.

Clint had tracked his share of men, but he wasn't stupid enough to think he was better at it than Mark Ordell, himself. He knew damn well that Ordell wouldn't leave any tracks if he didn't want to. Besides, the woods were such a mess of fallen branches, logs, leaves and animal tracks that Clint doubted he could find his pocket watch if he dropped it. Trying to pick out one man's trail would have been like trying to find a specific needle in a stack of more needles.

To that end, Clint tried to move as quickly as he could while doing his best to keep from being spotted himself. As he traveled, he kept a weapon in his hand at all times. Whether it was his rifle or pistol, Clint was always armed and expecting to be approached at any second.

There was no telling if Ordell was still in a sociable mood. At the end of the day, Clint still wanted to straighten out what he'd heard before simply believing it all and gunning for Ordell like those who'd already taken on that job.

Before leaving town, Clint had asked around a few places and found out that the mountain man and his two Indian partners had headed in the same direction that Clint had chosen. When he heard the snapping of twigs coming from somewhere ahead, Clint brought Eclipse to a stop and listened.

Sure enough, he heard a few horses stomping over what had to be some fallen logs. Clint wrapped Eclipse's reins loosely around a tree and circled around the source of those sounds. Just as he was about to take another step, he spotted a section of bushes moving against the flow of the wind.

He crouched down behind a tree trunk and froze.

That subtle bit of movement, which didn't match the way the rest of the bushes were moving, had been enough to mark the spot where one of the Indians stepped onto the narrow trail. He was the bigger of the two that had been with the mountain man and he stalked through the bushes like a creature half his size.

Clint had to hold his breath and focus on moving nothing more than his eyelids as he peeked around the tree. His muscles tensed and his heart sped up at the notion that he might be discovered any second. The Indian, however, moved effortlessly from one spot to another, gazing around with sharply focused eyes.

As Clint watched him, he remembered the mountain man calling that Indian Crow. As if living up to his name, the Indian glided past a branch where other birds were nesting without making enough noise to even draw their attention.

Clint's grip tightened around his rifle as Crow stepped behind one tree and practically disappeared from sight. When Crow reappeared, he was holding a tomahawk in his hand while carefully studying a spot not too far from where Clint was hiding.

And, like a bird that suddenly decided to take flight, Crow snapped his head in another direction and was gone.

Clint didn't dare move right away. For all he knew, Crow was circling around him from another direction. Possibly, the Indian was gathering up his partners before making his move. Or maybe he'd already moved along to another spot.

Clint still wasn't sure whether or not the mountain man and his partners could be trusted. He didn't even know what they might do if they spotted him. What he did know was that they would be a lot more use to him if Clint could see what they were doing without them knowing they were being watched.

More importantly, Clint's instinct told him to give those men a wide berth unless he wanted another fight. They'd already stepped up to him once with guns drawn. The next time was bound to end up a whole lot messier.

Clint had plenty of time to think about these things while waiting to hear or see another sign of Crow. All he heard was the wind rustling through the trees and all he saw was hundreds of branches swaying to a rhythm of their own.

TWENTY-THREE

As Clint headed back to where he'd left Eclipse, he stayed low and kept his rifle at the ready. The Darley Arabian was waiting patiently as if he knew only too well how important it was that he stay quiet. Eclipse barely even made a sound as Clint took his reins and led him back along the path they'd already taken.

As night drew closer, it was easier for Clint to find the other three men. The woods were getting denser to the north and it was impossible for three men to move through them without making a sound, no matter how skilled they were.

After tying Eclipse up again and scouting ahead on his own, Clint caught sight of a tiny flicker of light. He crawled on his belly through a thick mess of weeds and bottom-dwelling insects before finally catching sight of the other men's campfire.

The mountain man and Crow were huddled over the flame, which was barely large enough to produce enough heat to warm their hands. Something was cooking over the flame and after all the crawling he'd done, Clint looked at that cooking critter as if it were a king's feast.

He was forced to lie there and watch those two men eat

their supper for half an hour. Clint knew there was another Indian somewhere out there. Since he hadn't felt a knife in his back or been dragged off his feet just yet, Clint assumed he hadn't been spotted. That meant he had to stay put until he spotted that other Indian.

Finally, like a bobcat slinking in from the shadows, the other Indian stepped into the dim glow of the campfire and sat down. He spoke in a voice too soft for Clint to hear, while glancing up anxiously at every flutter of a bird's wing or rustle of a leaf.

The first opportunity Clint got to move was when the Indian stopped talking and started eating. Slowly, Clint backed away.

As hungry and cold as Clint was, he knew better than to build a fire when he got back to the spot where he'd left Eclipse. Even a flame half the size of the three men's paltry cooking fire would probably be enough to catch their attention.

Before long, Clint realized that just sleeping too close to their camp was taking a hell of a risk. Ignoring the gnawing in his belly and the chill digging underneath his skin, Clint took Eclipse's reins and led the stallion even farther back along the tracks they'd already put down.

He found a nice spot just over a quarter mile away that backed against a cluster of trees; not even a snake could get through. In front of him were more trees and bushes that started to look like one solid wall to Clint's tired eyes.

In the end, he wound up sitting with his back propped against a rock and a stick of jerked beef in his hand. He was almost too tired to chew the leathery meat, but it still felt good to get something in his stomach. With his rifle laying across his lap and his hand upon the grip of his Colt, Clint allowed his eyes to close and he drifted off to sleep.

●   ●   ●

Clint's eyes snapped open and his fingers tightened reflexively around the rifle when he heard something moving nearby. Even though his blood was racing in his veins thanks to the way he'd been pulled from his sleep, Clint felt as though he couldn't have drifted off for more than a few minutes.

Taking a glance upward, however, he saw the first hints of dawn spreading across the sky. Clint noticed Eclipse not too far away. It was clear the stallion wasn't in the spot from which the noise had come.

After getting his legs beneath him, Clint worked his way across the small clearing and into the thicker trees. Once there, he stopped and focused his eyes and ears to take in everything around him.

Although more birds and animals were moving about in the early hour of the new day, Clint couldn't hear anything big enough to cause him any concern.

He could see even less.

The trees were just as gnarled as they'd been the previous night and the ground was covered with just as much mulch. Other than that, the only difference was the hazy light filtering in through the branches over his head.

Clint thought back to what he'd heard and knew something had been stalking him. Something bigger than a rabbit or possum had made that noise, he was sure of it. For the moment, however, it was gone.

Realizing he had to be even more careful than he'd been before, Clint went back to the clearing, had a quick meal of dried oats for breakfast and got to work catching up with those other three men.

TWENTY-FOUR

Clint caught sight of the other Indian fairly early in the morning. With more than enough time to think, he remembered the mountain man calling that one Three. All Clint had to do was watch Three for a few minutes to figure out which way the Indian was traveling. After that, he led Eclipse a little ways back and then climbed into his saddle.

The woods had thinned out to make way for another section of Snake River. Now that he'd gotten a little breathing room as well as the noise of running water to cover him, Clint rode along the river and headed north into Oregon Territory.

Once he'd ridden for a few miles and figured he'd put some distance between himself and those Indians, Clint dismounted just long enough to do some hunting. He had no trouble whatsoever killing a few rabbits and he slung the animals over his saddle before moving on. The hardest part was not stopping right away to cook up the fresh meat.

When he did stop for the night, Clint made sure there was enough light in the sky to be of some use. There wasn't much more than a dark orange glow overhead, but it was bright enough that he didn't have to build a fire to see. He did pile up some rocks around a small pit which he dug out of the dirt to make a fire just large enough to cook the rabbits.

After getting some real food in his belly, Clint began to feel like a human being again rather than some animal scampering through the woods. Things were easier to see and his thoughts became much clearer as well.

All in all, he was doing fairly well. He should be able to reach the cabin the next day, which also meant Ordell shouldn't be too far away. If the other man didn't show up, Clint could always head for the nearest town with a telegraph office and ask Lisa Ordell for any more ideas.

For the moment, however, Clint was satisfied with what he was doing. He'd gotten the taste of that jerky out of his mouth and was convinced he'd gotten ahead of the mountain man and his two Indian partners. Clint even managed to wash his clothes in the river since they were caked with enough dirt and ants to start his own colony.

Letting out a breath and feeling the warm air brush over his chest, Clint actually started to let his muscles relax. Before he could get too comfortable, he heard the familiar sound of something moving through the trees. In fact, it reminded him of the very same sound that had woken him up that morning.

This time, Clint didn't act as if he'd heard it. He stayed right beside the cooking pit and prodded the piece of rabbit he was roasting as if nothing else was on his mind. Absently reaching for his canteen, Clint drew his pistol instead and twisted around to get a look behind him.

He found a slender, dark-skinned woman behind him, frozen like a deer caught in a hunter's sights.

"Come here," Clint ordered.

The woman did so without question. She was crouched down so low that her long, coal-black hair nearly brushed against the ground. Over her shoulder, there was a leather pouch decorated by a few beaded designs. Her clothes were made from smooth animal hides, which wrapped around her body like a second skin.

Her eyes were deep, dark brown and wide without displaying fear. The color of her skin as well as the angles of her features marked her clearly as an Indian. She moved toward Clint while straightening up just a bit until she saw Clint motion for her to stop.

"Who else is with you?" he asked.

She shook her head. "Nobody. I am alone."

"And you're just wandering around out here all by yourself?"

"Right now . . . yes. That is, until I found you."

"How'd you find me?"

"I saw you before," she said. "You rode away and I didn't find you again until now."

"So you've been following me?"

"Just for the day."

"Why?" Clint asked.

She looked away from him and started to sit down. Before settling in, however, she looked back up to Clint. He nodded and sat down as well since there wasn't a sign of anyone else in the area.

"Crow is my brother," she said. "I came to bring him food and blankets because the nights are getting cold."

"So he knows I'm here?" Clint asked, already dreading the answer.

To his surprise, she shook her head. "I did not tell him because they might hurt you if they knew you were near. They asked if I had seen a white man when I brought the food, but that was before I saw you. I know who the man is that they seek and it's not you."

"They're after a man named Mark Ordell."

"That's right. He is the white man who worked for the soldiers and killed many of our people. He killed most of my family. Howlett says you are after the same man."

"Howlett? Is he the man who travels with Crow and Three?"

She nodded and also smirked.

"What's so funny?" Clint asked as he found himself grinning as well.

The Indian woman's face was already pretty, but she turned absolutely beautiful with that little smile. "His name is Three Eyes, but Howlett only calls him Three. If he knew how close you were, Howlett might just call him One."

"That's funny. Speaking of names, what's yours?"

"In your tongue it would be Rain."

"That's very pretty."

"I brought you some food, but I can see you don't need it."

"You're welcome to some," Clint offered. "It's not bad, if you like rabbit."

She reached into her pouch and took out a few cakes that were about the size of biscuits. Handing them over, she allowed her fingers to brush against Clint's hand and slowly drag along his skin. She felt even softer than she looked.

TWENTY-FIVE

"The man my brother seeks is looking for him, Howlett and Three Eyes," Rain said. "I do not think he is looking for you. If you are seeking this same man, I think you will have an easier time finding him."

"If that's the case, I just might."

While Rain nibbled at a piece of the cooked rabbit, Clint ate one of the cakes she'd brought. It was a sweet mixture of corn, flour and sugar that melted in his mouth.

"The man is at a cabin not far from here," she said. "I think he'll be there for a while."

"I know where that cabin is. You're sure he's there?"

"Yes. I saw him there myself on my way here. I was not sure if I should tell my brother about it. He has been craving blood ever since my family was slaughtered. Part of me wants to go with him and kill the man who did those terrible things. Another part just wants to keep my brother from getting himself killed as well."

"Revenge tends to lead to a lot more blood being spilled."

"And you are not after revenge?"

Clint shook his head. "I'm out to learn what happened.

All I know is that a lot of innocent folks were killed and if this man was the killer, I can't just let him go about his business."

"He is the killer," Rain said. "I know because I saw him kill my people and cut the scalp from their heads. But that was a long time ago and no white men seem to care about it anymore."

"I care," Clint said. "Why else would I be out here in the woods when I could be in a warm bed by a roaring fire?"

"Because white men were killed, too," Rain replied. "That's why Howlett is on this hunt."

"Well, I'm not Howlett. No man deserves to be hunted and killed like an animal. No man and no woman, no matter what color their skin is. You hear me?"

Slowly, she nodded. The smile returned to her face, along with something else that Clint recognized. That extra something was the look of someone who'd just found what they'd been looking for. Clint had examined enough people's faces to know when he was being studied. And he could see that he'd just passed her test.

"I will help you," she said while nodding. "But only if you promise to not harm my brother."

"I've got no fight with your brother, but all of those men seemed ready to make a fight with me. I can promise to hold up my end, but I won't allow them to kill me."

"That is all I can ask." Holding her chin up, she said, "My brother will know better than to start a fight with an honorable man."

"Then there won't be a problem."

Rain got to her feet. "I must go back. Our village is a long way from here."

"Do you have to go so soon?" Clint asked as he stood and took hold of one of her hands.

Rain seemed hesitant at first, but then looked up at

Clint with that pretty little smile. "It will be a cold night. Perhaps it would be better if I stayed to keep you warm?"

"My thoughts exactly."

TWENTY-SIX

Rain's dress was all one piece and slid down over her breasts with just a few pulls from Clint's hands. Her dark nipples became hard the moment he touched them and she leaned her head back to let out a deep sigh. Soon, she was struggling to get her arms free so she could wrap them around the back of Clint's neck.

Clint moved his hands along the sides of her body, feeling the smooth curves of her waist and hips. Her body was warm and moved easily in his grasp. As he slid his hands up along her naked back, he could feel her hair brushing against his arms.

While savoring Clint's touch, Rain traced her fingers along his back and then worked her way to his bare chest. Soon, she was the one undressing him and she pulled Clint's jeans off while crawling back on all fours. She then spread out her dress and knelt on top of it, waiting for Clint to join her.

The sky overhead was a dark red as Clint once more wrapped his arms around the slender Indian woman. As her naked body pressed against him, she could feel his cock growing harder. Rain spread her legs just enough for his rigid penis to fit between them and start rubbing against the moist lips of her pussy.

Clint reached down to cup her tight buttocks and pull her in closer. After kissing her powerfully on the lips, he turned her around and cupped her breasts in his hands. She reached over her shoulders to play with his hair while Clint rolled her nipples between his fingers. Soon, she was leaning forward so that she was once more on all fours with Clint directly behind her.

For a moment, Clint looked down at the beautiful sight of Rain in front of him. Her black hair spilled over her shoulders and the supple line of her back curved perfectly to the slope of her raised buttocks. Rain turned to look at him over her shoulder, begging Clint with her eyes to not keep her waiting for one more second.

With one hand on the small of her back, Clint guided his cock between her legs until he found her tight, wet pussy. He eased into her just a bit, grabbed her hips with both hands and then slid the rest of the way into her.

Clint could feel her tremble with pleasure during that first thrust. The second time, he buried himself all the way inside of her, which sent an even larger shiver up Rain's spine. She pitched her head back and dug her fingers into the ground while lowering her shoulders and raising her backside to accommodate him.

Rain rocked back and forth, clawing at the ground and writhing as Clint pounded into her. She bit down on her lower lip to keep from crying out as Clint's rigid penis swiftly brought her to climax. When she felt her orgasm envelop her, she gathered up her leather dress and bit down on it until the sensation passed.

Clint could feel her muscles constricting around him and he drove all the way into her until she was trembling with pleasure again. When she looked back him this time, Clint saw an even greater hunger in her eyes.

"Sit down," she said.

Clint did as he was told and let Rain put him right where she wanted him.

"Now," she whispered, "lean back."

Supporting himself with both arms, Clint leaned back as Rain stood with her legs on either side of his hips and lowered herself down onto him. At first, it seemed that she might sit on his lap. Then, she spread her legs and leaned back until her feet were behind Clint and they were facing each other.

Rain supported herself with one arm and used her free hand to guide Clint's cock into her. As soon as he slipped past her moist lips, she eased her hips forward and took every inch of him inside of her. From there, Rain leaned back the rest of the way and used both arms to support her much like Clint was doing.

Both of them moved their hips in a slowly building rhythm. When Rain leaned forward, she could grind against Clint until he thought he would explode. When Clint leaned forward, he was able to thrust into her with sharp, powerful strokes.

They were both leaning toward one another when their orgasms came. Clint stared into Rain's eyes and pumped his cock into her. He could see her legs and arms trembling as her climax drained all the strength from her body.

Still hard despite his climax, Clint got to his knees and lowered Rain onto her back. He then got on top of her and rode her while Rain squirmed slowly beneath him.

A few hours later, she did some riding of her own.

TWENTY-SEVEN

Despite the fact that he was lying on the ground with his back to a rock, Clint woke up feeling rested and in good spirits. The first thing he noticed after opening his eyes was that Rain was no longer in the camp. That wasn't too big of a surprise. What did surprise him was the fact that he couldn't move.

Clint's arms were bound by something. His heart jumped in his chest. Looking down, he saw that he was wrapped snugly in a blanket woven from a thick cotton and decorated with Indian designs. Laughing at his initial reaction to Rain's kindness, Clint sat up and unwrapped himself from the blanket.

Just to be on the safe side, he checked through everything else in camp until he was certain Rain had left him just the way she'd found him. Even though his gut told him she had good intentions, it never hurt to double-check.

This time, like plenty of others before it, Clint's gut was right.

According to Lisa Ordell's directions, Mark's cabin wasn't far from the river. After finishing the cakes that Rain had left, Clint gathered up his things and followed the river north.

He knew Ordell could be tracking him at any time. For that matter, he knew Ordell could have been following him since he'd left Westerlake. But Clint also knew that Ordell was a good enough hunter to do his tracking without being seen. The only things that Clint could do was to be ready for when he was found.

Clint was ready.

There was no mistaking that part of it.

Even as he let Eclipse gallop along a stretch where the river roared over some high rocks, Clint kept one hand on his gun. When he didn't have his Colt ready to draw, he had his rifle out and lying across his lap. His eyes had even become better at sorting through the different kinds of movement that was always going on around him.

He no longer twitched when a small animal bolted from its den or a bird was flushed from its branch.

Clint had caught sight of a few movements he couldn't quite pin down, but didn't see enough to fire a shot. Rather than dwell on what those things could have been, he kept his eyes and ears open while riding toward Mark Ordell's cabin.

It was just past noon when he reached a bend in the river that Lisa Ordell had warned him about. Since the cabin was supposed to be near the bend, Clint doubled back a ways, climbed down from the saddle and approached the spot again on foot.

Keeping the rifle in his hands, Clint stalked through the trees and kept the sound of running water to his right. Before too long, the trees thinned out and gave way to a clearing with a small cabin pieced together from logs and sod right in the middle of it.

Clint stopped short of stepping from the thicker clumps of trees so he could take a careful look at that cabin. It was small enough to only have one room or possibly two very cramped ones. There were slits in some of the walls that were just the right size for rifle barrels to poke through, which would have been perfect for hunting any animals bold enough to step into the clearing.

At the moment, there wasn't any sign of life around the cabin and no barrels poking from any of those slits, so Clint moved carefully from the cover of the trees.

Every step of the way, he could feel his heart racing in his chest.

The closer he got to that cabin, the higher he raised his rifle. By the time he was close enough to touch a sod wall, the rifle was pressed against his shoulder and he was sighting along the top of its barrel.

Tentatively, Clint leaned forward and took a look through the closest slit. What little he could see through the narrow opening was marred by the dust set into motion from his own breathing. At the very least, he could tell there was nobody standing close to the wall. Clint kept his back to the cabin and slowly leaned to the side so he could get a look into one of the windows.

The glass was cracked and dirty, but he was able to see inside much better than he could through the rifle slit. He was right about there only being one room inside the sod walls. He was also right about there not being anyone inside.

Still keeping his guard up, Clint went to the door and pushed it open.

The hinges were well oiled and the only sound the door made was the bottom lightly brushing against the floor. Clint pushed the door all the way until its handle bumped against the wall. Only then did he step inside and start to do a quick search of the cabin itself.

All he found was a bare minimum of supplies and a small stash of food kept in a pantry on the wall. Clint opened a small bag of coffee and dipped his finger into it. The beans were still relatively fresh. There were also some strips of bear meat, which were enough to let Clint know that Mark Ordell had been there fairly recently.

Now that he had the information he'd been after, Clint

busied himself with making certain everything in the cabin was exactly how he'd found it. Every last bit of food was put in its place and every spare item lying about was set in its spot.

Clint was forced to sweep away the footprints he'd made upon the dusty floor, but was fairly certain the sod roof would drop enough fresh dust to put things right again.

After that, Clint left the cabin and did a careful search of the surrounding area. He found further evidence of Mark's presence in the form of fresh horse droppings near the river. Even though he looked around for other tracks, Clint didn't get his hopes up that Mark would leave any.

He wasn't too surprised when he found no tracks or even a broken branch to let him know if Mark was still nearby or which way he might have gone.

Clint did find something Mark left behind. It was a trap made from a large branch bent back into a tight bow with several sharpened stakes tied to the edge. Unfortunately, Clint only found the trap once his boot was caught up in the triggering snare.

TWENTY-EIGHT

Clint felt the snare as just a small tug on his right boot when he'd started to take his next step. Looking back on that moment, he didn't know if he stopped because of a last-minute suspicion that Mark might have set up a trap to guard his perimeter or if he'd spotted the snare from the corner of his eye.

It really wasn't that important at this point. Looking back on it, however, Clint realized that that one step had just made his life a whole lot more complicated.

The business end of the trap was the branch with the sharpened stakes. It was bent back so far that it nearly wrapped all the way around the tree to which it had been nailed. Each stake was at least a foot long and sharpened to a wicked point. The branch itself was at the height where, if sprung, it would catch Clint somewhere in his lower stomach or groin.

The longer Clint stared at the trap, the worse it looked.

And just when he thought it couldn't look worse, Clint noticed the thin rope used for the snare was snagged upon his boot. Clint tried to slowly move his foot back, but the rope only came with him. When he tried to set his foot down again, he felt the rope tighten and start to pull free from where it was laced.

Clint froze in an awkward position between steps. His left leg was bent and his right foot was lifted a few inches from the ground. Once he stopped moving, he could hear the creak of wood as the branch strained to straighten itself out.

"You've got to be kidding me," Clint muttered as he looked around for an easy solution.

By slowly lowering his foot, he was able to find what little slack there was in the snare. Unfortunately, there wasn't quite enough for him to set his boot all the way down. That was because his forward momentum had carried his leg just far enough to pull the snare completely taut.

Clint eased his leg back while keeping his foot over the ground. Even after he'd brought his leg back, however, the rope didn't come free. Gritting his teeth with frustration, Clint bent at the waist and reached down with one hand to try and pull the rope away.

His fingers gently closed around the snare, telling him immediately why he was having so much trouble.

Instead of a plain rope, the snare was actually a length of barbed wire with strands of rope wrapped around it. The rope was probably only there to keep the wire from glinting in the light. A little more checking told Clint that at least two barbs were snagged in the cuff of his jeans. One of them had even dug into the leather of his boot.

Testing the snare with his hand also let Clint in on another piece of news. The wire was too taut to have been simply strung across the path. It also resisted him too much when he tentatively tried to pull the barbs free. Clint took a moment to study the trap some more and found the spot where the wire was connected to the trigger holding the branch in place.

Right below the trigger, there was a counterweight just

large enough to keep the wire taut while still being easy to hide. That way, the trap could be sprung if someone pulled the wire forward and set off the trigger or if someone cut the wire and dropped the counterweight.

If he hadn't been standing on one foot, holding his breath to avoid getting impaled by several stakes, Clint would have been impressed by Ordell's ingenuity. It was a hell of a trap. Now that he'd been standing in that spot long enough, Clint could see a few more camouflaged snares strung at intervals farther up the path.

Suddenly, Clint felt himself start to wobble. Whether due to an odd breeze or just a twitch in his leg, he felt his balance shift and he immediately held out his arms to compensate. Clint was just in time to keep himself from falling, but he could tell he'd brought the snare to the brink of pulling the trigger.

The thought of those stakes slamming into him was more than enough to force Clint to adjust his weight and balance perfectly upon one bent leg. Somewhere along the way, Clint felt a sting in his ankle as if something had just bitten him.

As much as he would have preferred a beetle in his sock, Clint knew that the barbed wire had just eased through the leather and clamped down on his boot. It was a miracle the trap hadn't been sprung. The creak of the branch was only getting louder. It was just a matter of time before it snapped forward.

Clint pulled in a few breaths to steady himself.

He tossed the rifle he'd been holding behind him and focused his eyes upon the branch with those stakes lashed to it.

Easing his arm to his side, Clint slowly bent his right knee and stretched his left leg to the safest possible spot.

He could feel his supporting leg begin to strain and his knee grow warm with the effort of holding all of his body's weight. He could also feel his other leg start to cramp up after being held in such an awkward position for too long.

Clint struggled to keep his eyes from focusing upon the wooden stakes and the nasty tip each one of them possessed. He did his best to keep from thinking how terrible the pain would be if even one of those spikes were driven into him. He tried not to think about how long he would be lying there after getting impaled before anyone might find him.

Clint pushed past all of those things and focused instead upon the branch to which those stakes were tied. He couldn't make out exactly how the branch was being held back, but Clint could see the wood was taxed to its limit and was too strong to break.

After letting out a breath, Clint crouched down a bit lower, gathered up his strength and then pushed himself backward from that one leg.

As he dropped toward the ground, he stretched out the leg that was snagged in the barbed wire, just to give him as much extra time as possible. The trigger had already been pulled, however, and the branch let out a creaking groan as it snapped forward. Those stakes sliced through the air right until Clint plucked the Colt from his holster and fired off a quick shot.

Aiming more on reflex than anything else, Clint pointed the Colt like he would point his finger. He didn't even know if his bullet hit the mark until after his back had slammed against the ground.

Through the rush of blood in his ears, he could hear the snapping of wood followed by the heavy thump of the branch landing in the bushes beyond the tree.

Clint forced himself to open his eyes and reflexively patted himself down. There was nothing impaling him, which brought about a loud sigh of relief.

The branch was now just a jagged stump and was still smoking after being cut by hot lead.

Clint lay in the spot where he'd landed as if waiting for another device to be sprung. The next thing that concerned him was the sound of his shot still rolling through the air. If Ordell was in the general vicinity, it was a safe bet he'd heard that shot.

Before getting up, Clint reached down and pulled the barbed wire that was still lodged in his boot. Sure enough, that damn wire even managed to catch in his finger before coming free.

Clint fought the urge to shoot the wire just to make himself feel better. Instead, he started checking around for more traps so he could prepare for Mark Ordell's arrival.

TWENTY-NINE

Ordell arrived with as much warning as a shadow gave when it crept along the ground. He slipped in through one of the patches of trees that looked too thick to cross and somehow did it without stirring more than a few stray leaves.

His face was smeared with blood and dirt, turning it the same color as his long, gnarled beard. The big man stopped like a buck testing the edge of a lake and then took a few cautious steps toward the cabin. His eyes darted back and forth, soaking up every last detail of the clearing.

When he approached the cabin, he stopped at a spot between the door and window as if he were somehow able to stare through the wall. Finally, he leaned to one side and took a quick look through the window. Without even trying the door, he continued his search of the paths leading away from the clearing.

Almost immediately, he spotted a patch of ground indicating where Clint had headed. There wasn't much more than some dirt and a few pebbles on the ground, but Ordell saw enough there to put a smile upon his face. His eyes traced the path that Clint had walked, ending right at the spot where his trap had been sprung.

Ordell held his rifle in both hands and straightened up a bit as he walked toward his trap. Nodding to himself as he pieced together what must have happened, he grinned even wider when he saw the exposed length of barbed wire.

Slowing his steps as he approached the tree, he reached out and ran one fingertip along the spot where the deadly branch had been broken. Ordell then heard the rustle of leaves, but was too late to move before the pistol barrel lowered itself down to his head like a snake dropping from its nest in the tree.

"Hello, Mark," Clint said as he reached down to hold the Colt to Ordell's forehead. "I was wondering when you'd show."

Ordell froze in his tracks, in much the same way that Clint had done when he'd felt his boot snag upon that wire. His eyes flicked up to follow the pistol all the way up to the arm that was holding it. From there, he could barely make out the spot where Clint had nestled himself in the tree just over the sprung trap.

"You the one I almost got in that trap?" Ordell asked.

"Sure am. That was a hell of a device."

"Thanks. I came up with it myself. You're the first to get out of it."

"I'm honored."

"So, you gonna stay up there or are we gonna talk like two men 'stead of one man and a cat?"

Rather than give his answer in words, Clint dropped down from his perch and landed with just a slight stumble. Since he hadn't given Ordell a warning, Clint was able to steady his aim again before the other man could make any sort of a move against him.

"What's the meaning of this, Clint? Do you really need to point a gun at me?"

"I don't know. From what I've heard, you're a pretty dangerous man. Speaking of which, drop the rifle."

"I could say the same about you," Ordell replied as he tossed the big gun into the bushes. "Fact is, your reputation's got a whole lot more color than mine."

"I'm not here about my reputation. I'm here to get the facts about you."

"If this is about Josh, I already said my piece on that."

"Fine," Clint said. "Then maybe you could tell me about Ed Gray or those Indians that you scalped."

"Scalpin' ain't illegal if it's the army that pays for me to do it."

"That doesn't make it right, either."

Ordell let out a breath and straightened to his full height. Hooking his free hand over his shoulder, he said, "I got some perfectly good chairs in that cabin. How about we head in there to talk?"

Clint shook his head. "Considering how well you've got this area trapped, I'd rather not take a chance to see what surprises you have inside."

"All right, then. You're the one that came all the way out here. You're the one that climbed a damn tree and waited up there for God knows how long so you could say what you needed to say. Just say it and be done with it. I've got things to do."

"Tell me about Ed Gray," Clint said.

"He was a selfish prick who got what was coming to him, just like those filthy redskins who I scalped. Is that what you wanted to hear?"

"Only if it's the truth."

Ordell cocked his head to one side and thought it over for a few moments. "Actually . . . it is the truth." Once he saw that Clint didn't have anything ready to say to that, Ordell asked, "Now what?"

"And what about a man named Howlett."

"He's dead, too?"

"No. How do you know him?"

Ordell shrugged. "I got into a disagreement with a few of his friends. Maybe a family member or two also. It's been a while, so I don't honestly recall every last detail."

"What sort of disagreement?" Clint asked.

"They wanted to stay alive and I disagreed."

"This isn't a game, Mark."

"Isn't it? Ain't every part of life just one big game? Ain't it a gamble whether or not we make it through disease and every other manner of hell that's out there just so we can grow up?"

"What are you trying to do, exactly?" Clint asked. "Talk me into your idea that killing is all just some kind of game like everything else?"

Ordell's eyes widened hopefully and he smiled. "Yes! I knew you'd understand."

"Leave that kind of bullshit for the philosophers. Better yet, run it past a judge and see if it gets you out of a murder charge."

Nodding slowly as his smile faded, Ordell shifted on his feet. "I've got a gamble for you. I'll bet that you won't shoot an unarmed man in the back."

Tensing as he saw Ordell turn around, Clint took a step back so he would be out of range if Ordell tried to take a swing at him. "Don't do this, Mark. I'd rather not kill you, but I will."

Ordell acted as if he didn't hear a word Clint said. He even acted as if he didn't know a gun was pointed at him. Instead, he kept his hands at his sides and started walking slowly down the path and away from the cabin.

As a warning that no man could ignore, Clint thumbed back the hammer of his Colt. The distinctive metallic click rattled through the air like a snake's rattle. "You want to explain yourself? You'll have all the time in the world to talk on the way back into town."

"In front of a judge and a jury box full of pasty-faced worms? I'd rather get my judgment out here."

"Suit yourself."

"Or I could keep on gambling."

Clint's stomach clenched as he sighted along his barrel and lined up a killing blow.

"I bet you're not willing to take your chances with the rest of these traps just to catch me."

Lowering his aim a couple of feet, Clint squeezed his trigger and sent a round intended for Ordell's leg. Instead, the bullet hissed through empty air since Ordell had leapt into the bushes the moment his last word had escaped his lips.

Clint's impulse was to chase after him, but he quickly remembered the other trip wires he'd seen when he was stuck in that barbed wire. Looking down that path, he could still see those snares and could only imagine what was out there that he couldn't see.

Swearing under his breath, Clint backed up and let Ordell go.

THIRTY

No matter how much he could have cursed himself out for not putting a bullet into Ordell when he had the chance, Clint choked that down so he could wait and watch for Ordell's return. The hunter had dropped his rifle and there was no way in hell the man was going to leave it behind.

Clint put his back to the cabin and watched the bushes. Before long, he felt his muscles tense and lock into position. His breathing slowed so he could hear every last thing that was going on around him. Soon, he had a real good idea of what Ordell felt when he was hunting.

Not wanting to turn his back for a second, Clint stayed in that spot and waited. He knew the hunter would be back. No matter how many other weapons Ordell might have had, he would go back for that rifle. Ordell thought like a warrior and that gun was more than just a rifle to him. Much like Clint's pistol was more than just another Colt.

After a while, Clint's senses became so sharp that he could practically hear the leaves scraping together with every breeze. That's what made it so strange when he heard absolutely nothing at all where Ordell was concerned.

Tentatively, Clint inched his way toward the bushes. He kept his body low and one hand stretched out in front of him so he could feel for any more snares or other possible traps. Thinking back to what he'd seen and what Ordell had said, Clint felt like a fool.

The thought hit him like a sharp, sudden rap on the nose and it caught his attention in a similar fashion.

There were definitely other traps out there, but Ordell knew Clint was wary of them. That's why he'd put it in Clint's head to be afraid of them as if every tree were rigged to turn against him after one misstep. It was the worst kind of bluff: the kind that had a kernel of truth at its core.

Although he kept on the lookout for more traps, Clint didn't let that prevent him from doing what needed to be done. He had to find that rifle, since it was one sure piece of bait that would draw Ordell straight back into Clint's sight.

Unfortunately, Ordell's bluff had held up just long enough.

The rifle was nowhere to be found.

After waiting and then searching for over an hour Clint had to admit defeat. He might not have seen exactly where it had landed, but the rifle was too damn big to disappear under some bushes. It wasn't there, plain and simple. Clint had to admit that no matter how much it stung.

Clint stood up in the bushes and looked around. When he saw nothing but more shades of green and brown, he shook his head and let out an exasperated breath. That rifle was big and Ordell was bigger, but somehow both of them had snuck out right from under his nose.

Backing out of the bushes, Clint went to the cabin and dropped down into the same spot where he'd been waiting before. This time, he sat with his legs stretched out in front of him and his head leaning back against the wall.

He was tired.

At that moment, that one fact was all that could enter Clint's mind. He was tired and every muscle in his body ached. He'd been put through the wringer and every last bit of it chose that second to rush up on him. The thought crossed his mind to just let Ordell keep running and scamper through his woods.

Men killed each other all the time and Ordell was just another one. He killed and one day he'd probably be killed. No matter what Clint did about it, that same story would repeat itself with other names filling the leading roles.

Those thoughts lasted just about as long as the one that had told him to shoot Ordell in the back and be done with it.

Clint knew he didn't have much of a chance of making everything right but he did have a chance to set this one thing straight. So long as he did what he could when he could, he knew he'd be able to meet his maker with a clear conscience. After taking a few minutes to catch his breath, Clint got up, dusted himself off and got his mind back on track.

Right about then, like a reminder that no good deed went unpunished, Clint heard the sounds of men approaching from every direction besides the one in which Ordell had gone.

Clint positioned himself at the front of the cabin with his back to a wall so he could watch as many of those directions as possible.

The first one to emerge from the trees was the Indian known as Three. He glared at Clint with pure death in his eyes.

"Well, well," Howlett said as he stepped forward. "Looks like you showed your true colors after all."

THIRTY-ONE

Clint was on his feet and ready for anything by the time the second Indian stepped out of the trees. All three men took a position around Ordell's cabin and didn't seem too disappointed to find Clint there instead.

"If you're looking for Ordell," Clint said, "he just left."

"We'll find him," Howlet replied. "But you'll do just fine for now."

Clint steeled himself and took a closer look at the other men. There was something different about them somehow. They had a meaner look in their eyes as if crawling through the dirt and hunting like animals had made them into animals themselves.

Then again, perhaps that look was in their eyes because they saw those same things in Clint.

"One man already got killed for jumping the gun like this," Clint said. "There's no need for you men to force my hand again."

Howlett planted his feet and narrowed his eyes. "Or maybe we didn't jump the gun. Finding you here, waiting for your friend Mark Ordell has made me feel like a fool for letting you get away the last time."

"He's not my friend. I was damn near killed in one of his traps."

"You look fine to me."

"I guess if you found me nailed to one of those trees, you would've believed me?" Clint let out a sigh and waved off the other men. "Forget it. I'm too tired to argue with another hardheaded mountain man."

Both of the Indians looked back and forth as if they were waiting for the first shot to be fired. Crow had a tomahawk in each hand and Three carried a shotgun with a charm and some feathers tied to the barrel. Those weapons were gripped tightly and slowly brought up in preparation for whatever came next.

Howlett, on the other hand, lowered his rifle. After that, he started to laugh. "You do look tired, I'll give you that. But why the hell should we think you ain't working with Ordell?"

"I don't know," Clint sighed. "You could always start off with the fact that I'm sitting here rather than tramping around the woods right along with him."

"Are you a lawman?"

"Do you see a badge pinned to me? Or a posse, for that matter?"

"Then what the hell are you doing out here?" Howlett asked.

"I'm bringing Ordell in to answer for what he's done. If you men lost so much because of him, you'd do well to help me instead of trying to stop me."

"No," Three said. "The man who killed my people must die. White man's laws do nothing."

"There's plenty of dead men who've swung from a noose that would disagree with you," Clint replied.

"Then why not just kill him ourselves rather than string him up so a bunch of townsfolk can watch?" Howlett asked.

"Because that's the proper way it's done."

Until now, Crow hadn't moved more than the swaying branches of the trees behind him. When he moved more than that, it happened quicker than a bowstring snapping forward after being let go. The Indian's left arm snapped back and then out again to let one of his tomahawks fly through the air.

The heavy weapon turned end over end one complete rotation before slamming into the wall next to Clint's head. Although he was able to draw his Colt and take aim, Clint knew he would have been dead if Crow had intended on targeting his head rather than that wall.

"You won't bring that animal from these woods," Crow declared. "He will die for what he's done and he will die in these woods."

"And where's the justice for the others Ordell killed?" Clint asked as he kept his gun at hip level. "You three get to avenge your losses, but what about the other folks and their losses?"

Crow's eye twitched and he slowly brought up his right arm. The tomahawk he carried was slightly smaller than a hatchet and had a narrower blade. The handle was carved and smoothed down to allow it to cut through the air almost as well as the blade cut through everything else.

"If you thought I was such a danger, you would have killed me with that first throw," Clint said.

"He may be swayed by your words," Three snarled. "But I am not."

"This is your chance, mister," Howlett said as he held an arm out to keep Three from making another move. "Leave now and stay the hell out of our way. If we cross paths again and you try to keep us from doing what we need to do, you're a dead man."

Three gritted his teeth and started to bring his shotgun up once more. He wasn't able to take his shot before Mark Ordell took his.

The sound of the rifle was unmistakable. It exploded

through the air like a crack of thunder and sent its round past the heads of all four men as it tore a loud path over Howlett's shoulder, past Three's nose and between the faces of Clint and Crow.

The four men ducked low and looked in the direction from which the shot had been fired. All they saw was the thick tangle of trees between the cabin and the river.

Another unmistakable sound was Ordell's own voice. "Fer a bunch of damn killers," he shouted, "you sure do a lot of talking!"

Three looked like an enraged wolf as he bared his teeth and fired his shotgun toward the sound of Ordell's voice. Even as he ran and fired a second time, Three was digging fresh ammunition from a pouch on his belt.

When Clint glanced toward the sound of movement beside him, he found Crow standing less than a few inches from his face. He reflexively brought his Colt around, but stopped short of pulling the trigger. Crow met Clint's eyes and retrieved his tomahawk from where it had been lodged in the side of the cabin. After that, Crow let out a sharp cry and headed into the bushes.

"Hot damn," Howlett said with a grin. "Looks like the hunt is on."

THIRTY-TWO

Clint rushed to pick up his rifle before charging after the other three. He could hear the Indians' war cries echoing from the direction of the river, followed by a few shots taken here and there. Even though he couldn't see what was going on, Clint knew well enough that those shots were wild and probably didn't hit a thing.

Although he didn't think Howlett and the Indians would catch up to Ordell right away, Clint knew those men had spread out far enough to keep Ordell from circling back to the cabin right away. Ordell's taunt had been like a spark against kindling, which meant the hunter wanted a chase. Clint wasn't in the mood to disappoint him.

As he bolted down the narrow path leading to the river, Clint tried to think a few steps ahead of Ordell. What surprised him the most was how quickly he was able to put himself into the hunter's frame of mind. After the last few days, Clint had learned some hard lessons from Ordell. Now was the time to put them to use.

Crow ran with his body leaning forward and low. His hands were wrapped tightly around his tomahawks and his arms were swept back against his sides like a raven's wings. As

127

he leapt forward, he looked three steps ahead for any trace of the man he was after.

In his ears, the Indian could hear the screams of his family as they were killed and maimed by the butcher he pursued. In his mind, Crow could imagine what Ordell had done after hunting those innocents down like so many rabbits.

He didn't have to imagine the fear in his family's eyes when their time had come. He'd seen it plenty of times in his nightmares.

Crow caught sight of something that didn't belong. It was a length of root that was stretched perfectly straight from one bush to another and it was too high off the ground to have grown there on its own. Even though he recognized it as a trap, Crow was moving too swiftly to avoid it. At the last second, he hopped up and over the snare without so much as grazing the false root.

A few steps later, Crow felt something tug against his ankle and then snap. It must have been another snare, but Crow hadn't seen it. He felt the bite of something slicing into his leg, however, and heard something moving swiftly toward him through one of the nearby bushes.

Crow was still running at full speed and his feet were digging into the ground to try and push him faster. He caught sight of the branch swinging toward him and knew instantly that it was one of those same traps that he and Howlett had found along the way to the cabin.

Since the branch was on his right side, Crow swung that arm forward and twisted his wrist to give his tomahawk a bit of extra power. He felt his blade smack against something immediately and kept his arm moving despite the sting he felt in his shoulder.

A sharpened stake dug into his flesh and ripped a gouge in his right bicep. The gouge was shallow, however, since Crow managed to deflect the branch before it did any real damage. When he took his next step, his tomahawk cut all the way through the branch and he felt the stakes bump against his leg as it fell.

Knowing that traps like these were the reason Ordell had been so bold, Crow smiled and kept running. Ordell was going to have to do much better than that if he intended on winning this battle.

Howlett didn't bother looking straight ahead. Instead, he kept glancing to the trees on either side. He didn't bother looking for the traps, since he already had seen how good Ordell was at hiding those damned contraptions.

Instead, he looked for odd shapes connected to those trees or even a patch of leaves that were just a bit too thick on their trunks. Those were the traps themselves, and Howlett didn't have to see any more than that to know which trees were safe and which to avoid.

The moment he spotted one of those traps, he dodged to the side and slowed his pace just to make sure he wasn't about to kill himself. He might not have kept up with the Indians, but Howlett's slower pace was good enough to catch sight of Ordell.

It seemed the hunter was banking on everyone running at him the same way. After lighting the fuse, Ordell seemed to have stepped to one side so he could watch the explosion. Howlett was shocked to see the other man so quickly. Judging by the look on Ordell's face, he was just as shocked.

Both men swung their guns to their shoulders and took aim. With all the commotion going on around them and with both men moving on their own, it would have taken a small miracle for them to aim properly. As he'd figured, Howlett's shot punched through a tree trunk while Ordell's whistled through the air overhead.

Howlett grinned, knowing that Ordell's relic of a gun should take at least double the amount of time than his to reload. While working the lever of his rifle, Howlett stopped and took a moment to aim. Since Ordell didn't have the sense to move, it seemed as though the hunt might be over sooner than Howlett expected.

Before Howlett could squeeze his trigger, another plume of black smoke erupted from Ordell's barrel. When he saw that smoke, Howlett was certain it would mark his last moment on earth. He was wrong.

When he blinked again, Howlett saw Ordell pointing his rifle straight up into the air. Crow was directly beside Ordell with one tomahawk still lodged on the underside of the hunter's rifle.

Since there wasn't any time to think about how close he'd come to dying, Howlett took a breath and lowered himself to one knee. If he was going to repay Crow for saving his life, now was a good time.

Before Howlett could take aim, however, he heard a shot from the woods nearby.

THIRTY-THREE

Even as he felt the rifle get knocked out of one hand, Ordell managed to keep hold of the trigger and grip. The rifle roared and spat its shot into the air before Ordell finally saw the hand that had knocked it loose. "Son of a bitch," he snarled while taking hold of the rifle once more and pulling it down.

Crow stared up at him defiantly from a low crouch. One of the Indian's hands was still sweeping upward after forcing the rifle up. His other hand was sweeping around in a tight semicircle to send his other tomahawk through Ordell's stomach.

As his fingers started to curl around the rifle's barrel, Ordell brought the stock down and around to viciously crack the Indian in the head. His fist clenched tightly around the barrel and began a second swing when another rifle shot blazed through the air and tore through his cheek just a few inches shy of a killing blow.

Ordell reeled back, but instinctually managed to keep hold of his rifle. It was also instinct that brought his rifle up just in time to block an incoming swing from Crow's tomahawk. Ordell caught the tomahawk right under the blade,

131

lifted the rifle over his head and yanked the weapon from Crow's hand.

The tomahawk pitched through the air and Crow watched it just long enough to see where it might land. He then swung his second tomahawk, but only sliced through empty air before the butt of Ordell's rifle caught him in the temple. After that, Crow was too dizzy to chase anyone.

As he ran, Ordell hunched over and held his rifle like a spear. A shotgun blast ripped through some trees to his left, telling him exactly where that second Indian was. Ordell grinned to himself and pointed the rifle barrel toward the ground.

After a few more steps, Ordell felt his rifle barrel scrape against wooden planks that had been hidden beneath a layer of leaves and branches. He leapt over the boards, pulled himself down low again and ran doubly fast.

"I saw him!" Three shouted as he sent another shotgun blast toward the spot where Ordell's head had popped up.

Howlett had seen him, too, but didn't bother taking a shot. Instead, he quickened his pace to try and catch up to Ordell rather than waste ammunition shooting at fleeting glimpses. He knew he was on the right track when he heard leaves rustling directly in front of him. The next thing he heard was a loud series of snaps, which was made by something much heavier than branches. In fact, it re- minded him of a roof caving in.

Howlett was running at close to full speed when he heard a sickening thump followed by a loud scream.

Everything in Howlett's mind told him to stop running. His legs dug into the dirt, but his momentum carried him another few feet before sending him right over the edge of a pit roughly the size of a door.

Howlett let out a surprised curse as he felt his feet slide into the pit. He threw his rifle away and desperately scram- bled with both hands to grab hold of anything at all that would stop his slide. One set of fingertips dug into the earth and wrapped around a clump of weeds. His other hand managed to clamp onto the ground itself and dig in with every bit of strength he had.

His eyes were clenched shut and his teeth were gnashing together as he waited to slip and fall. Although his boots were scraping against something below him, he wasn't about to slide another inch. He was grabbing onto the ground so tightly, it would have taken a team of oxen to pry him loose.

Now that he'd come to a stop, Howlett sucked in a few breaths to gather up the strength to pull himself out of the pit. Between breaths, he could hear a wet gurgling sound along with what sounded like a whimpering animal.

Howlett twisted to look behind and beneath him and saw Three lying at the bottom of the pit. The hole itself looked to be as deep as a grave. Considering the fact that the bottom was littered with sharpened stakes, a grave was exactly what it had become.

The Indian lay wedged among those stakes. A few of them were jabbing into his stomach and chest, but there had to be plenty more that were wedged in so deeply they couldn't even be seen.

"You all r—" Howlett cut himself off before asking one of the stupidest questions of his life. Forcing himself to look at Three's face instead of his grievous wounds, he asked, "Are you alive?"

Three sucked in a breath and let it out with another agonized groan. He tried to talk, but could only let out a gasp that trailed off into silence. The best thing Howlett could hope for was that the Indian was already dead.

Kicking against the tops of those spikes, Howlett pulled himself up and strained every muscle in his arms and shoulders in the process. As he was bringing his legs back over the edge, he heard someone rushing toward the pit.

"Slow up!" Howlett shouted. "It's a trap."

The steps stopped immediately and were replaced by a slow, deliberate rustle. A few seconds later, Crow's face emerged from the bushes. The instant he saw Howlett, he rushed forward and helped the man back onto solid ground.

"Where's Three Eyes?" Crow asked.

Howlett glanced over his shoulder and said, "He's in there. He's dead."

Crow looked anyway. His face darkened as he saw the body. When he looked back again, it seemed another ghost had taken residence behind his eyes. "Where did Ordell go?"

"I don't . . . I don't even know," Howlett gasped.

"And the other white man?"

"If he's still alive, I wish him luck. He's sure as hell gonna need it."

THIRTY-FOUR

Clint didn't even bother trying to run through that thick tangle of trees and bushes. If Ordell was going to go through the trouble of announcing himself to a bunch of armed men intent on killing him, there was no reason to assume those trees weren't even more dangerous than the ones where Clint had almost been impaled.

Still, thinking like a hunter wasn't enough. Clint knew Ordell wasn't just a hunter. He was a hunter who reveled in the kill. That small detail was enough to give Clint an idea of where to look for his own prey.

Clint stuck to the one spot where most trackers wouldn't think to look for a man like Ordell. That spot was the trail that led back to the river and it was out there on an open stretch of road that Clint caught sight of the very man he'd been looking for.

Emerging from the trees like a badger, Ordell was hunched over to half his size and scuttling forward in a quick waddle. The smile on his face made it seem like he was in the middle of a game of hide-and-seek.

Half a second before Clint could do anything, Ordell turned and squeezed off a round from his rifle. Knowing all too well what that rifle could do in the right hands, Clint

135

jumped to one side and then dove behind a tree. The shot cut through the air over Clint's shoulder, coming amazingly close to drawing blood.

"That you again, Clint? I was hoping you weren't the one that landed in that pit."

Clint leaned from behind the tree and saw Ordell scurry into the bushes. "What is it you want to accomplish, Ordell?" Clint shouted. "You don't really think you'll make it past all these men, do you?"

"I'd say I got a better'n average chance. 'Specially since there's at least one less man to worry about. Just listen to him scream, Clint. When a man's at the bottom of a pit full a spikes, it's hard for him to sound much like a man anymore. Sounds more like a woman to me. Maybe he caught a spike or two in a tender place."

Clint ducked back and forth behind his tree, taking quick looks for Ordell without staying exposed for too long. Sure enough, he could hear the screaming Ordell was talking about. And, sure enough, he couldn't tell who it was that had gotten hurt. One thing he knew for certain was that the man was hurt awfully bad.

"Come on, Clint. Come after me," Ordell taunted as if reading Clint's mind. "Come after me so you can brag to those bleeding men how you snagged the big prize."

Clint could still hear the screaming, but now he could hear Howlett's voice as well.

"Slow up!" Howlett shouted. "It's a trap."

When he spoke again, Ordell already sounded as if he were farther away. "Come on, Clint! Let's finish this up proper!"

At times, Clint had wondered what the hell would cause a man to kill the way Ordell had killed. The fact that Ordell had committed those terrible things of which he was accused wasn't even a question any longer. But there was no more time to think about what made a man do what Ordell did. All Clint thought about now was making the man stop.

Pulling in a breath, Clint jumped out from his cover with the rifle pointed directly in front of him. Keeping the pained screams behind him, he fired at the first thing that moved in front of him.

He fired, levered in another round and fired again. Clint stuck to the road and fired at anything big enough to make a noise or move a branch. His hands worked at a blistering pace until it seemed that the rifle in his hands wouldn't be able to keep up.

Clint could feel the heat pouring from the rifle's barrel as he fired and fired until the last round had blazed into the trees. After tossing the rifle away and drawing his Colt, he stood his ground and waited for another target.

Once the thunder of those gunshots had cleared, Clint couldn't hear anything else but the dwindling cries of whoever had been hurt. At that moment, Clint made his choice and decided to help who he could help instead of playing more of Ordell's game.

He kept his Colt ready as he made his way through the trees. Clint had no trouble finding the spot where the others were, since there was plenty of motion and noise to draw his attention. Before he got close, Clint made sure to announce his arrival by speaking loudly and clearly.

"Hold your fire. It's Clint Adams."

Even after that, Clint was nearly cut down the moment he stepped into Howlett's and Crow's sight.

"Where's Ordell?" Howlett asked. "Did you see him?"

"I saw him for a second or so, but that's it."

"Then why the hell didn't you go after him? If that asshole gets away, all of this will be for shit!"

"It sounded like you needed some help," Clint said. "Since it's too late to get Ordell right now, I suggest you take whatever help you can get. Who's hurt?"

Howlett was lying against a tree with his legs stretched out in front of him. "Never mind that!" he snarled. "Ordell's right around here! I saw him with my own eyes. I won't have Three dead for nothin' by letting that murdering crazy man skip out of here!"

"I chased him as far as I could and he went straight into another batch of trees just like this one. Since his own cabin isn't far away, I'd say he's had more than enough time to booby-trap this whole damn place. Now, if you want to go running into that, be my guest. I heard someone get hurt and I know it's in one of those traps. Tell me where he is!"

Howlett let out a tired sigh and nodded toward the pit. "Three was the one making the noise, but he's done now."

Clint leaned forward just enough to see the bloody tips of a few spikes. "Is he still in there?"

"Yeah, but like I said before, he's done. I was nearly in there with him."

Crow stumbled into the little clearing and then hunched down on one knee as if he were paying his respects to the dead. One of the Indian's hands was pressed to his head and a small trickle of blood was coming from his temple.

"What about you?" Clint asked. "Are you all right?"

Without looking up, Crow replied, "I will be fine."

"He tussled with Ordell," Howlett explained. "Caught a nasty knock from the butt of the bastard's fancy rifle."

"Can you move?" Clint asked.

"I twisted an ankle and nearly yanked an arm out of its socket, but I should be all right. I'd be a hell of a lot better if Ordell was dead right about now."

"Ordell won't be going anywhere. After all the trouble he went through today, I doubt we'll have to wait too long before seeing him again." Kneeling down beside Howlett, Clint placed a hand on the man's shoulder and could immediately feel where some of the bones were out of place. "Come on, let me help you back to your camp."

"I don't need any help."

Clint stepped back and watched the man try to get to his

feet. Howlett managed to get halfway up before wincing and gritting his teeth in pain.

"You just gonna stand there?" Howlett grunted. "Or are you gonna help me?"

THIRTY-FIVE

Howlett wasn't lame by any stretch of the imagination, but he'd twisted his knee and ankle in his fall. Even though he needed some help getting back to camp, his injuries weren't enough to drain the fight out of him. In fact, he seemed just as ready to fight Clint as he was to fight Ordell. Howlett kept right on fighting until he was dropped back into his own camp.

Landing with a thump, Howlett grunted and spat out a string of obscenities.

"You're welcome," Clint said.

"Might as well put a bullet in my head if I can't run after that son of a bitch," Howlett growled.

Clint was already busying himself pulling down thick branches. "You're going to be fine. You don't have anything that a splint and a bit of rest won't cure."

"Really? And when am I supposed to rest? The bit of time before that animal comes after me again or the bit of time after he picks me off?"

Now that he had the lengths of wood he was after, Clint looked for some rope. He found some looped to the saddle of Three's horse. "That's just the pain talking. Here"—he took a bottle he'd found in one of Three's saddlebags and tossed it over to Howlett—"take a few drinks of this and calm down."

Still glaring at Clint, Howlett pulled the cork from the bottle and tipped it back to his lips. After letting some of the firewater pour down his throat, he lifted the bottle to the sky in a quick salute. "That Indian may have been crazy, but he fought the good fight."

"Speaking of Indians, where's your other partner?"

"He ain't here?" Howlett asked while looking around at the small camp. "Considering how long it took for you to get me back, I would've thought Crow had been here, had supper, taken a nap and gone back out again."

"I thought I made good time, considering I was dragging a complaining sack of bones like you along with me."

Howlett took another drink and grinned. "All things considered, it was a hell of a run. That's the closest we got to that crazy son of a bitch since we started."

"We'll get another chance," Clint said as he set down the wood and rope he'd collected. After forming a splint from the branches and tying it around Howlett's ankle, Clint started to wrap the rope around a spot above Howlett's knee, but got his hand swatted away.

"I can finish it up myself." Howlett grunted. "Lord knows it ain't the first time I mended myself."

Clint took the bottle from Howlett's hand so the man could tie off the top of the splint. Although he didn't usually prefer whiskey, Clint shrugged and took a sip from the bottle. After everything that had happened, the drink went a long way toward making him feel like he wasn't still running.

"Where do you think Ordell got to?" Howlett asked.

Clint shook his head and took one more sip before putting the cork back in the bottle. "Right now, I don't even care."

"How can you say that? After everything, you're ready to quit?"

"No, but I'm not going to turn myself inside out trying

to figure out every noise I hear and dream about which tree Ordell might be hiding behind. That's exactly what he wants. Besides, he's still out there and he's still a flesh and blood man. He'll need his rest, too."

"He is still out there," Crow said as he stepped into the campsite.

Although they were startled by the Indian's sudden appearance, Clint and Howlett were too tired to jump.

"Where've you been?" Howlett asked.

"Putting Three Eyes to rest."

"You pull him outta that pit?"

"I buried him where he fell. His spirit is free and his body is now one with the earth. That is all that matters."

"What matters is that we get the sick son of a bitch who dug that pit," Howlett said. "I seen plenty of men die before, but that was . . . that was inhuman is what it was."

Since he'd come back to the camp, Crow had yet to take his eyes off of Clint.

"What's the matter?" Clint asked the Indian. "You still don't trust me? You think I put on a good show and am still working with Ordell?"

"You weren't with us when we chased him," Crow pointed out. "I don't know where you were."

"I wasn't drawn into chasing him through a series of death traps that Ordell had rigged before we even got there," Clint replied. "That's why you didn't see me. Hell, I would've even warned you about them if you would've bothered to ask. I would have even said something when Ordell drew you men into the trees, but you three bounded off like a bunch of rabbits."

Crow straightened up and narrowed his eyes into angry slits. In a matter of seconds, the fire inside of him dwindled and he nodded slowly. "You could have killed us both when you found us."

Judging by the startled look on his face, Howlett hadn't gotten around to thinking about that just yet.

"Now you're thinking straight," Clint said.

"Yeah," Howlett said as he chuckled nervously under his breath. "That's what I figured all along."

"So, you will be hunting with us?" Crow asked.

"No."

Howlett and Crow both looked at Clint as if his answer had come in another language.

"What do you mean no?" Howlett asked.

"Just what I said," Clint replied. "Looking at this like a hunt is giving Ordell exactly what he wants. After everything I've seen so far, my guess is that he set this up a long time ago and worked awfully hard to draw you men to this spot.

"Ordell has hunted men for years and has been paid handsomely for it. Josh Ordell found out that much and was killed. Something's been bugging me about that, though. Mark Ordell can come and go as he pleases by just walking out of town and disappearing into the trees. There's only one good reason for him to kill his nephew when it would be no problem for him to just pick up and head somewhere else.

"This hunt," Clint said. "Right here and right now. He's had this all set in motion for a while. If Josh started talking about it or if he'd gotten the law involved or even if he got too many folks poking around in this patch of woods, Mark wouldn't have been able to have his fun."

"Son of a bitch," Howlett groaned. "We've been led by the nose for so long and I never saw it until now?"

"When you were tracking Ordell, did you follow mistakes he'd made or bodies he'd left behind to show you where he was?" Clint asked.

Howlett didn't answer directly, but the mix of anger and shame on his face spoke volumes.

Clint looked over to Crow and said, "What happened to your people was enough to gather the best warriors and hunters you knew to send after Ordell. It's a horrible thing to have done, but it suited his purposes perfectly."

"In the eyes of an animal," Crow said through gritted teeth, "there is no good or bad. I believe you are right in these things you say, except for one thing."

"What's that?" Clint asked.

"I knew this killer wanted to hunt me. If the animal wishes to put his neck in front of my weapon, I am willing to step into his den."

"Yeah, but walking out again is the tricky part."

THIRTY-SIX

Clint walked back into his own campsite and felt oddly at home. The spot wasn't much more than a little clearing in a good location with a small pit dug for a fire. Still, it was quiet and close enough to the river for Clint to wash off his face and take a cool drink. Eclipse stood beside him, sipping from the river like it was just another day.

"I'd give every cent I have to have your worries right about now," Clint muttered as he patted the Darley Arabian's nose. "Then again, I wouldn't be too crazy about eating fried oats and sleeping in a stall."

Perhaps Clint was tired or perhaps he'd been out in the woods for too long, but he suddenly thought that was one of the funniest things he'd ever heard. Perhaps he just needed to laugh for a few seconds, because that alone made him feel a whole lot better.

After leading Eclipse back into the campsite, Clint sat down and stretched his legs out to enjoy a few moments of quiet. A few moments was all he got before he heard soft footsteps padding toward him. His hand drifted toward his gun, but he didn't draw. Instead, he sat and waited until the soft footsteps stopped.

"It's all right, Rain," he said. "Come on over here."

The Indian woman stepped into the campsite and made her way quickly to Clint's side. She sat facing him with her legs drawn in tightly and her knees held close to her chest. "You have a good nose to know it was me," she said.

"More like good ears."

"It is the sign of a good hunter."

Clint groaned at the sound of that last word. "It comes from too much practice doing things I'd rather not be doing." Seeing that he'd only put confusion onto the Indian woman's face, Clint shook his head and said, "Never mind. What brings you here?"

"I wanted to make sure you were all right. I heard that . . ." Lowering her eyes for a moment, Rain had to gather up some strength before saying, "I heard that Three Eyes is dead."

"You heard right."

"Ordell killed him."

"Three killed himself by charging without thinking," Clint said with a bit of an edge to his voice. "And if it had been another sort of trap, he might have killed someone else."

"He was always too ready to fight. Crow said that is why he made it this far in hunting down Ordell."

"I'd rather not think about all of that right now."

Setting her chin upon the tops of her knees, Rain asked, "Aren't you worried that Ordell will find you?"

"Not really."

"But he is a great hunter. Crow says he thinks Ordell already knows where Howlett made his camp."

"He probably does know," Clint said. "He might even know where I am right now, but I don't think he'll come into this clearing with guns blazing. I doubt he'll even fire a shot at me for a while."

"Why not?"

"Because that's not part of a hunt." Looking at her, Clint could see genuine concern on Rain's face. He could also see plenty of fear. "He is a great hunter. He laps it all up like milk. The hunt, the kill, the chase, even him being chased. He loves all of it and he wouldn't bring it to an end just by firing off a few shots from afar. That's how boys hunt. At least, that's probably how he sees it. I didn't see much of him today, but I saw enough to show me that he's loving every minute of this.

"Besides," Clint added, "we gave him a good run today. He'll need to lick his wounds for a while."

"You've said that before."

"Have I? Well, it's still true."

Averting her eyes just a bit, Rain said, "And you wouldn't be able to stop him if he decided to come here anyway."

"I wouldn't put it quite like that, but you're not far off the mark."

"When I was a child, I was told the same thing about the soldiers that would come to our villages."

"Well, just because you can't keep someone from crossing your path," Clint said, "doesn't exactly mean you're about to let them roll right over you."

Rain smiled and said, "That's what my brother would say when he would hunt down the soldiers who killed my people for sport. You remind me of my brother."

"Not too much, I hope."

"You have his fighting spirit," she quickly amended. "That's all I meant."

"Maybe you should go see your brother. I think he could use the sight of a friendly face right about now."

"He is gone already," Rain said while slowly shaking her head. "I spoke to him for a little while, but he didn't have much to say. He told me about what happened to Three Eyes and how close you all came to killing Ordell. After that, he didn't want to talk anymore."

"He didn't really strike me as the sort who would take a moment to catch his breath. Although, I hope he knows that running prey to the point of exhaustion is an old hunter's trick and Mark Ordell is most certainly an old hunter."

"I don't know anything I could say to make him stop, even for a moment. He will go after this man until he can no longer move." Shifting her voice to a deeper, more stern tone, she added, "Only then will he rest."

"You've already had this conversation with Crow before?"

"Many times. That is why I have been following him. Every now and then, I can get him to smile or eat more than a few bites."

"That's very thoughtful. He's a lucky man to have a sister like you."

"He's not the only lucky one, you know," she said while slowly crawling onto Clint's lap. "I'd like to make you feel good for a while. They say a woman can make a man's eyes sharper and his blood run hotter."

Clint wrapped his arms around her and slid his hands along the curve of her back. "I can certainly vouch for that second part."

THIRTY-SEVEN

As she undressed him, Rain worked her fingers along every inch of Clint's body. She massaged his tired muscles and peeled away the clothes so she could keep her hands moving upon him. He leaned back and let her do what she pleased, feeling more like a human being instead of an animal running through the woods.

Clint watched her run her hands along his chest and stomach. He then reached up to peel the top of her dress down to reveal her pert little breasts. Rain's dark nipples were already growing hard and when Clint rubbed them, she let out a trembling sigh. With a few shrugs of her shoulders and wriggles of her hips, she squirmed out of her clothing and then tossed her hair over her shoulder.

Looking down as she opened his jeans, Rain glanced back up at Clint just as she slipped her hand between his legs. She rubbed his hardening cock and breathed in deeply as she felt him become fully erect. She begged him with her eyes to strip down the rest of the way and when he did, she guided Clint's penis between her legs.

Rain kept her hands flat against Clint's chest as she rode him. Her legs pressed tightly against him and she kept her head bowed forward so her hair would brush against his

149

skin. Rocking back and forth, she began grinding her hips and digging her fingernails into his flesh.

Clint could feel the strength in her body the way he could feel power in a bowstring. Her muscles were taut and her breathing was fast and getting faster with every stroke. Placing his hands upon her hips, he held her in place as he started pumping into her.

The moment she felt him take charge, Rain let out a gasp and leaned back until she could grab Clint's ankles. The front of her body formed a slender arch and her stomach became tight as a drum while she savored the feel of Clint sliding in and out of her.

Now Clint only had to hold onto her with one hand. His fingers curved around her hip and felt her tight backside. He moved his other hand up and down along the front of her stomach to feel her muscles move as she breathed. Slowly sliding his fingers down again, Clint placed his thumb on her clitoris and started moving it in a slow circle.

Rain's eyes fluttered open and her pussy tightened around him. She let her head fall all the way back as every muscle in her body began to tremble with a powerful orgasm. As the climax slid through her, she pumped her hips up and down over Clint's cock until he drove it in as deeply as it would go.

Clint sat up and Rain bolted up to meet him. Her arms wrapped tightly around him and she held on until her climax was finished. When she could finally take a breath again, Rain got up and pulled Clint to his feet.

"Come here," she whispered.

"Where are you going?"

Rain walked across the camp to one of the largest trees at the edge of the clearing. Placing her hands against the tree, she arched her back and turned to look at Clint over her shoulder. "I want to make you feel as good as I do."

No more explanation was necessary. Clint took a moment to savor the sight of Rain's slender, naked body standing in front of him. Her black hair brushed against smooth, dark skin. The curve of her spine made a gentle slope right down to the tight roundness of her buttocks.

As Clint stepped up behind her, he felt Rain arch her back a little more and spread her legs a bit farther apart. His rigid cock fit easily between her legs and slid perfectly back into her wet pussy. Just sliding it halfway into her was enough to make Clint let out a contented sigh.

Looking down once more at her backside, Clint put his hands on her hips and drove into her again. This time, he thrust forward until he was buried completely inside of her. His first few pumps were long and slow, easing almost completely out of her before sliding back in. Then, he gave in to his own desire and started thrusting harder.

Rain grabbed onto the tree and watched Clint over her shoulder with wide eyes. Soon, she was moaning and tightening around him once more as she was brought into a second orgasm.

Holding her little body in his hands and feeling her pussy envelop him perfectly, Clint only had to keep thrusting before he felt his own pleasure reach a boiling point. He placed one hand on her shoulder and slid it down her back. By the time his hand came to a rest upon her backside again, he was exploding inside of her.

"Was that good?" she asked while turning around to lean back against the tree.

"The best."

Rain lifted one leg up to wrap around Clint's waist and pull him to her once more. "I think I can do better."

THIRTY-EIGHT

Ordell had never felt better in his life.

Even though he was caked in mud from head to toe, felt every muscle he owned burning under his skin, and hadn't had a mattress under him for weeks, he couldn't remember ever feeling better. The dirt smelled better than rosewater to him and the cold of the morning was only beaten by the chill of the night.

Even the blood encrusted into his beard wasn't enough to dampen his spirits. On the contrary, it was more like a mask that had been placed upon him so he could play out his final role. The Indians could paint up their faces for war, but they'd never look as fierce as Mark Ordell wearing his dirty, bloody smile.

His camp was situated under a low rock shelf close to the river. It was cold. It was wet. It was also home to plenty of bugs and lizards, but that only meant it was the sort of place none of the others would think to look for a camp. It was also located perfectly between the other two camps, allowing Ordell to move back and forth so he could keep an eye on Clint, Howlett and those other three Indians. Well, now there were only two.

Ordell grinned a bit wider as he felt the bloody crust on

his left cheek crack. Scooting closer to the open end of the rock shelf, Ordell leaned down close to the water so he could get a look at his face. His thick beard was caked with more than just dirt and leaves. Now, there were thick clumps of dried blood as well as a few bits of charred flesh.

As he pulled out some of the bigger pieces, Ordell thought about the shot that had given him that wound. It had come from the one man he'd never intended on being here for this hunt. Ordell could still see Clint Adams taking aim and firing his shot as if the whole thing had been captured like a photograph in his mind.

Feeling that bullet tear through his face had surprised the living hell out of Ordell. It had also been a great reminder of why he hunted in the first place. Although tracking down prey and delivering the killing blow was one of the best things a man could feel, Ordell knew that victory was only made sweeter when there was the danger that he might be killed along the way.

Finding Howlett and those Indians was no work at all. They caught Ordell's eye after just a little bit of looking. Riling them up had been even easier, since Ordell had found a way to make some money in the process.

Preparing his cabin and laying all of his traps had been a labor of love. Ordell thought back fondly to whittling every last one of those stakes while sitting on his porch and watching the sun set. He thought about it even now as he stuck his fingertips into the wound in his cheek.

The gouge in his face nearly went all the way through and Ordell admired Clint's shot the way a fellow carpenter would admire another man's hand-carved dining room table. That wasn't an easy shot to make. Ordell knew because he'd dodged dozens of shots taken by men in the middle of a hunt.

Most men fired their guns as if they were blindly flailing their arms during a saloon fight. Their shots were wild and desperate. Actually, they were pathetic, but Ordell knew all too well that every animal would fall victim to their instincts sooner or later.

Every now and then, however, a man could push through the fear and choke back the urge to run just long enough to win the day. Most men wouldn't even have the guts to keep quiet while threading a needle and sewing up their own face and staring at their reflection in bloody water.

Ordell held back his beard and scrunched his mouth to one side as if he were merely shaving as he pushed his needle through his cheek again and again. Every bit of pain made his eyes sharper and his nose pick up more smells from the air.

Most men couldn't appreciate the smell of blood, especially if it was their own. Ordell, on the other hand, never knew he could run so fast as when he'd felt Clint's shot rip through his face and the smell of blood fill his nostrils. There was even a moment when Ordell had wondered if Clint would be able to chase him down and deliver the killing blow.

Ordell paused as he was about to tie off the last stitch. Finally, he shook his head. Clint might be a hell of a runner and even a hell of a fighter, but he wouldn't be able to close the book on Mark Ordell. Not unless he was able to get a clean shot with that fancy Colt he wore.

Just thinking about going up against Clint Adams on even ground made Ordell gnash his teeth together. Surely, those others had been spreading the word about all the things that had been done to flush them from where they'd been hiding. Clint seemed like the sort who might even sign on to the sob stories spit out by those Indians.

But it had been Josh who'd truly pushed Clint into this mess. That young prick who would've turned on his own uncle seemed to have a use after all. Until this moment, Mark had almost forgotten about the kid. There had been a quick moment of satisfaction when he'd pulled his trigger, but that had passed.

Josh deserved to die. Killing him was just something that needed doing. There had been no honor in it. There was no challenge. It was just a simple case of killing a dirty piece of vermin.

But Clint had come after Mark more than once regarding Josh. For that, Ordell almost wanted to thank the kid for serving at least one use in his miserable, ungrateful life.

"Thanks, kid," Ordell said under his breath.

The Indians liked talking about ghosts and spirits, but Ordell didn't hear anything that could be a spirit's voice. All he heard was the water flowing over the rocks and his heart beating in his chest.

Josh was gone, so Mark put the kid out of his mind.

Cupping his hands, Ordell dipped them into the water and made certain to scoop up some of his blood in the process. The Indians also talked about the power of blood and how it made a man stronger. They painted their faces with it sometimes.

Drinking down that water, savoring the coppery taste of his blood, Ordell felt his heart beat faster. Apparently some of those savages' superstitions were correct. Ordell decided he would try talking to Clint Adams's ghost once this hunt was over.

THIRTY-NINE

The sun's first rays had yet to make it through the trees in the thickest portions of the woods. Even at that early hour, plenty of animals were out and about. Most of those animals were on four legs. Three of the biggest, however, were on two.

Howlett grunted and grumbled under his breath as he struggled to get up and get some water from his canteen. He grunted and grumbled some more as he fixed some coffee. The moment he picked up on the sound of snapping twigs, however, the grumbling stopped and a wide smile crossed his face.

Dropping the kettle and coffee grounds he'd been holding, Howlett snatched up his rifle and aimed at the woods. This time, he didn't grumble one syllable as he shuffled into the trees. When he saw Rain's face, he lowered the rifle and grumbled some more.

"Damn it, girl, I could've killed you."

"Where's my brother?"

"Crow ain't hardly been around here the last day. He only comes by to eat and let me know what he's found when he goes out scouting."

Rain's eyes widened a bit with a glimmer of hope. "He's been eating?"

"Sure he has. Next time you come into camp, watch where you're stepping. It took me a good while to set up them sticks just right to let me know when someone gets close."

"If I could see your traps," Rain asked, "wouldn't that make them useless?"

Howlett furrowed his brow for a moment and then started waving his hand as if he were swatting at a horsefly. "Goddamnit, just help me set them things up again!"

"I brought a message from Clint."

"Really? Why didn't he come and talk to me himself instead of just walking away like he did?"

"Because this way Ordell has to watch two camps instead of just one."

Once more, Howlett's brow furrowed. This time, he seemed to be more pleased with the results. "That's pretty smart. Did you think of that on yer own?"

"No. He said you would be complaining about him not telling you where he went."

"What's the message, smart-ass?"

An hour later, Howlett met up with Clint at a spot less than a mile from Ordell's old cabin. The grizzled man had already gotten used to walking around with his splint and he moved close to his old speed with just a limp to show for it.

Clint waited at the agreed-upon spot with his Colt strapped around his waist as always. Beyond that, he carried his rifle in one hand and a knife strapped to the outside of his boot. When he saw Howlett coming, he asked, "Where's Crow?"

"Hell if I know. That Injun's been worked up for the last day. I think he's wound up tighter than a cheap watch."

"Then maybe it's best for him to keep his distance."

"You and I think the same way," Howlett said. "I'd rather split up the reward money for bringing in that killer with you than I would a red man."

"That's not exactly what I meant."

"Still, it's something for you to think about."

"Were you followed?" Clint asked.

Howlett let out a ragged breath and went through a long process, which ended with him sitting on the edge of a stump. "Who can tell?" he grunted. "I'm too damn tired to care anymore. All I know is that I'm ready for whenever that chicken shit Ordell decides to show his face again."

"You sure woke up on the right side of the bed this morning."

"Bed of rocks is more like it, and I'm damn ready to get back to a real bed. What do you think about my offer as far as the reward money goes?"

"Let's just try to get Ordell," Clint said. "After that, we can discuss what to do when it's over."

"Make up yer mind quick," Howlett grumbled as he started walking away. "That ain't the sort of offer that keeps for very long. Why'd you want to see me, anyways?"

"Ordell's hurt. If we're going to close in on him, now's the best time."

"He's hurt?" Howlett asked as he straightened up to pay attention. "Are you sure about that?"

Clint nodded. "I fired the shot myself. It was yesterday during our little dustup with him and those traps."

"How bad was he hurt?"

"I don't know for sure. He still got away from me, so it's nothing too serious. Even so, I know I drew blood because there was plenty of it left behind. I was aiming high, so it's got to be on his head or shoulder. Even though it may not have put him down, any wound will stir him up. And when someone gets stirred up—"

"They make mistakes," Howlett said. "Good thinking.

If we work together, we might just be able to catch up to him when he's still good and mad."

"Which is why I wanted to have a word with you. Perhaps if we start beating the bushes, we can flush him out and take him down. It's definitely better to get this done sooner rather than later. The longer we stay out here, the more we're playing his game."

"I agree. I sure as hell don't want to give him time to set up more of those traps."

"You've got to be able to find Crow," Clint said. "All of us need to work together to get this job done."

"To hell with that Injun. Let's get started and if he finds us, he can take part. I doubt you'll be able to talk much sense into that one anyways."

"Fine. You head to the south and I'll head to the north. If we both circle in toward the west, we should meet up."

"Hopefully, we'll catch Ordell in between us."

"It's a start."

"And a damn good one," Howlett said. "It's a pleasure working with ya rather than against ya, Adams."

"Hopefully we can swap hunting stories over a beer when this is done."

"If we both make it through this, the drinks are on me." With that, Howlett pulled in a breath and got moving to the south. He quickly disappeared as the narrow trail took a turn behind a tall old tree.

Clint watched him go and then started walking in the opposite direction. The trail was a sorry excuse for a path and deteriorated more into dirt tracks between tree stumps. Clint walked for less than twenty minutes before he heard someone moving alongside of him. There were so many trees in that direction that he couldn't tell if it was a man or animal, but whatever it was, it seemed to keep pace with him.

Raising his rifle to his shoulder, Clint aimed in the direction where he'd last heard the sounds and waited.

Crow exploded from the bushes a few yards from where Clint had been aiming. The Indian moved so quickly that Clint wasn't able to adjust his aim before one of Crow's tomahawks was at his throat.

"I hear you're looking for me," Crow snarled.

FORTY

The modified Colt hung at Clint's side, but was completely useless to him at the moment. Even the rifle in his hands wasn't going to do him much good since the sharpened stone blade of the tomahawk was already pressing against the exposed flesh of his throat.

"I was looking for you, Crow," Clint said. "But that's no reason to come at me like this."

"I heard you and Howlett talking. While I track the man who killed my people, who killed Howlett's people, who killed countless other people, you try to cheat me out of my part of the reward money."

"This isn't about a reward. I came out here to bring an end to Ordell's hunting, not chase after some reward."

"Then why talk behind my back about that money?"

Clint gritted his teeth and shifted on his feet so he could get a better look at the Indian. "The first thing I asked Howlett was where I could find you. The only reason anything was said behind your back is because you were nowhere to be found. Secondly, Howlett's the one who brought up the reward at all. If you have something to say about the money, say it to him."

Suddenly, Clint raised the stock of his rifle in a short,

upward arc. The end of the gun caught the tomahawk right behind its handle and knocked it far enough away from his neck for Clint to take a step back and turn to face the Indian.

"And third," Clint said, "I've had more than my fill of being ambushed. You're real lucky I didn't shoot you out of gut instinct."

Crow already had his shoulders squared and his body settled into a fighting stance. He'd kept hold of his tomahawk and even brought the weapon around as if he intended on taking a swing at Clint. Instead, he straightened up and relaxed a bit.

"Fine," Crow said. "I am not hunting this man for the money, but my part of that reward is rightfully mine. The remains of my family can use that to buy their land back from those who would take it."

"I didn't know about the reward until you and Howlett brought it up. That's not why I'm here."

"Then why did you want to talk to me?"

"We need to work together to get Ordell."

"I thought we were working together," Crow said.

"I mean working on the same plan, not running through these woods looking for the same man. If we just get our heads together on a simple course of action, we can save ourselves from crossing paths, covering the same ground a dozen times and jumping at each other's footsteps."

Nodding, Crow said, "I heard you say as much to Howlett. That is a good idea."

Clint sighed and lowered his rifle. "Jesus, Crow, that's all there is. No need to make a production out of it."

But the Indian kept staring at Clint. His fist tightened even more around his tomahawk and his chest rose and fell like a set of bellows with every powerful breath. He started to talk a few times, but couldn't get the words out. Finally, he said, "That is not all."

"I'm listening."

"You have seen my sister."

Nodding, Clint said, "I have. Rain's been relaying messages and she even brought me a blanket."

"She has spoken of you."

"And?"

Crow's nostrils flared as he sucked in a breath through his nose and let it out from between clenched teeth. The muscles in his arm twitched as he slowly brought his tomahawk up to waist level. "You have . . . been with her. Haven't you?"

"I know she's your sister, but Rain's a grown—"

"You've been with her! You've disgraced her!"

Taking a step back, Clint made sure he was out of Crow's reach. "You're making too much out of this. We've got plenty to worry about besides whatever happened with—"

"I know what happened!" Crow snarled. "And if I am here to avenge my family, I will not stand by to let you rut in the dirt with my sister like some kind of dog."

"Nobody forced anything to happen, Crow. Don't you force this or you won't like how it turns out."

But the Indian's eyes were wild and he now had his tomahawk up to cock it back. "I cannot see Ordell, but his time will come. I can see you right now and I won't wait one more minute to deal with you."

Opening his hands, Clint let the rifle slip from his grasp and drop to the ground at his feet. "If you want me to fight, you'll have to wait. I know you're not the sort of man to attack an unarmed man."

If Clint's gesture had any effect, it was impossible to say. In fact, it seemed as if Crow hadn't even noticed that Clint's hands were now empty and held out to either side.

Clint tried to think of what he could say to calm the Indian down. The longer he looked at the wild expression on Crow's face, the more Clint realized there was nothing he or anyone else could say to smooth things over. All Clint could hope for was that Crow would put this aside until he was thinking clearer.

That hope was quickly shattered.

Crouching down while taking a step back, Crow snapped his arm back by his ear like a catapult getting ready to spring. He let out a battle cry and started bringing his arm forward, leaving Clint no other choice but to draw his Colt.

Clint leaned to one side as his hand flashed down to his holster. Even though he meant to dodge Crow's tomahawk, he cleared leather before the weapon even left Crow's hand.

The Colt barked once and sent its lead through the air.

Crow reeled back with his arms flying to either side and his fist still wrapped around his tomahawk. One shoulder smacked against a tree, sending him sideways to the ground. The Indian landed behind a bush and remained motionless.

After waiting a few seconds, Clint angrily shoved his Colt back into its holster and snatched up his rifle. "God-damnit, Crow," he growled under his breath.

Since there wasn't anything else for him to do, Clint continued on his search and headed north.

FORTY-ONE

Rain sat huddled in the bushes, too frightened to move a muscle. She crouched like a rabbit that was seconds away from getting its head caught between the teeth of a wolf, praying that she would go unnoticed.

She'd heard Clint talking to her brother and meant to step in. After hearing the edge in Crow's voice, however, she knew better than to try and calm him down. He would only have pushed her aside and told her to leave. No matter how much she would have tried to beg Clint to step back and make peace, she doubted he would have listened.

Both men had had their minds made up and there was nothing to be done about it.

All Rain could do was stay hidden and watch as the two men butted heads. When she'd heard the shot from Clint's Colt, every muscle in her body had jumped. Her hands snapped up to cover her mouth before she made a noise or cried out.

Her hands were still pressed against her mouth when she looked over to see another figure huddled in the brush.

Mark Ordell crouched down until he barely seemed to take up more space than Rain. His hat was drawn down tightly over his head, leaving nothing but the tip of his nose and a tangle of beard to protrude from beneath it. One hand was resting upon his knee and the other held his rifle just an inch or two off the ground, so most of the long barrel and stock was beneath the top of the grass.

The hunter didn't move in the slightest. Rain watched and waited to see if he would attack or try to pounce on her, but the man simply didn't budge. The only way she'd noticed him there was because he was a shape in her line of sight that hadn't been there the last time she'd checked.

Even though his eyes were mostly hidden from her view, she could tell he was watching Clint intently. His posture leaned toward the spot where Clint stood as if he were about to spring forward at any moment.

Even though his beard covered his mouth, Rain could tell Ordell was smiling. The curve of his face was shifted upward and, if she watched carefully, she could see the hairs closest to his lips moving with his silent laughter.

When Ordell moved, it almost made Rain jump. She'd been watching him so closely that she'd stopped expecting him to budge.

Ordell's head barely shifted. It was barely half a twitch, but the twitch was in her direction. That was more than enough to tell Rain that she'd been spotted.

Slowly, Ordell shifted to look at her face-to-face.

Rain felt a cold knot form in her stomach when she saw the way Ordell's beard had been torn apart on the left side of his face to reveal a twisted, bloody stretch of gnarled skin. The wound looked even worse due to the blood that was still clumped into his beard like an extension of the gash itself.

Ordell raised the hand from his knee, held up one finger and then held that finger to his lips.

Rain did what she was told and stayed quiet as Ordell shifted and moved away.

FORTY-TWO

Clint rarely thought about the odds of himself surviving a fight. Doing so was a good way for a man to get himself killed. Quite simply, the odds never favored a man when he drew his gun or took his knife from its sheath. There were a hundred things that could go wrong and any one of them could cost a hell of a lot.

But as he made his way through the woods and examined every blade of grass for a snare, Clint had more than enough time to think about his odds. No matter how much he had in his favor, there was no possible way the odds could go his way.

This was Ordell's battleground and Clint was a damn fool to fight him there. Unfortunately, Clint also knew that if he didn't face Ordell here and now, he might never catch up to the hunter again.

Ordell could come and go as he pleased and if he decided to disappear, Clint could only rely upon a miracle to finish up this business. After all the blood Ordell had spilled for little or no reason at all, there was no way Clint was about to let the man get away with it.

Even though it meant playing Ordell's game on his own ground, Clint couldn't just walk away. The only way for him to have anything at all in his favor was to try and push a few of his own rules into the game. Even then, he wondered if he could win.

The steps he heard coming from behind him were rushed and close together. Clint's first instinct was that it was an animal that had been flushed out to run in his direction. When he heard the breathing coming from the one making those steps, Clint knew it wasn't from any animal.

Turning around, Clint sighted along his rifle and lowered himself to one knee. When Rain came into view, Clint met her like a one-man firing squad.

"Is anyone behind you?" Clint asked without taking the rifle from his shoulder.

Rain was breathless as she kept running. Even seeing the gun in Clint's hands wasn't enough to make her slow down until she was close enough to hold him. "I don't think he's chasing me, but he was right there."

"Ordell?"

"Yes. He was right there and I didn't know until it was too late."

"Where was he?" Clint asked. "Where were you, for that matter?"

"I wasn't far from where you were talking to my brother. I heard the shot and I heard someone fall and—"

Taking hold of Rain by her shoulder, Clint grabbed her tightly and forced her to look directly into his eyes. When she still kept looking around wildly, he gave her a gentle shake and asked, "Where was he?"

"He was listening to you."

"How much did he hear?"

"I don't know. I didn't see him at first but then he was just . . . there. I didn't even hear him coming."

"Did he try to hurt you?" Clint asked.

Rain pulled in a deep breath and forced herself to let it out slowly. Once she did, she felt Clint's hand loosen from around her arm. "He didn't try to hurt me. He didn't even come near me. All he did was look at me and . . ." As she spoke, Rain pictured Ordell in her mind. The wound on his face seemed even more gruesome and she imagined what his eyes must have looked like under the brim of his hat.

"And what?" Clint asked.

Lifting a trembling finger to her lips, Rain imitated what Ordell had done. "He did that," she said. "And then he left. Once I knew he wasn't coming for me, I ran."

"Was he hurt?"

That snapped her out of the nightmarish visions flowing through her head. Her eyes snapped back into focus and she looked at Clint. "Yes. His face was bloody."

"Could it have been a bullet wound?"

"Yes. That must have been where you shot him."

"I know. I was kind of hoping for something a little better."

"It looked pretty bad."

Clint shrugged. "Didn't seem to slow him down at all. Besides, someone like Ordell probably wears his scars like medals."

Rain was quiet for a few seconds as Clint started walking along his route. She kept up with him easily and even began looking for traces of Ordell along with him. Before too long, she asked, "Where is my brother?"

"You said you were there. Didn't you see where he went?"

Rain shook her head. "I heard the shot and I heard someone fall. All I could see was a few shapes on the other side of the trees."

"We shouldn't be talking about this now," Clint told her.

Nodding slowly, Rain kept pace with Clint for a few more minutes. Suddenly, she stopped and held out an arm to get Clint to do the same thing.

"What is it?" he asked.

She silenced him with a sharply raised hand. Holding her head up toward the tops of the trees, Rain eventually closed her eyes completely so she could focus entirely on the sounds around them. When she opened her eyes again, she lowered her hand and then pointed off the trail to the west.

Recognizing the haunted look in Rain's eyes, Clint brought his rifle up and whispered, "Do you hear him?"

She nodded, but only hesitantly. That was enough for Clint to know that she wasn't entirely certain about her warning.

A week ago, Clint never would have been able to hear the subtle shifting of something in the bushes that he could right now. It was a sound that would have been mistaken for the wind blowing through leaves to the inexperienced ear. This sound had some weight behind it, though. It was a small yet important difference that he'd been forced to recognize during the course of Ordell's hunt.

Running the tip of his finger along his rifle's trigger, Clint waited to hear that sound again. When he did, he sighted a few paces ahead of it and fired.

That shot was answered by an even louder shot, which was unmistakably from Ordell's rifle.

Clint dropped to one knee and pushed Rain behind him. "Get out of here and find someplace safe to hide."

"When should I come for you?"

"As soon as the shooting stops."

FORTY-THREE

Rather than play mouse to Ordell's cat, Clint gritted his teeth and made his best guess as to where Ordell was hiding. He then fired in that direction while running to the southwest. He stuck to the trails as much as possible. Every so often, he heard another shot from the hunter's rifle whip through the air.

There were times when Ordell would stop shooting, but Clint knew better than to relax. Instead, he kept firing and heading southwest. When he didn't have a notion as to where Ordell was, Clint fired into the air just to cover the sound of his own footsteps.

Finally, he made it back to a bend in the river, which was the biggest open spot he'd found in all the time he'd been in those woods. Clint got behind the biggest rock he could find and quickly reloaded his rifle.

"What's the matter, Clint?" Ordell shouted from somewhere close by. "You gettin' tired?"

"Actually, I'm getting thirsty. Why don't you come on over and we can have a drink?"

Ordell's laughter echoed over the water, making it difficult for his position to be nailed down. "I'll have my drink after the hunt's over, but I'll be sure to raise a glass in your name."

"What the hell did I ever do to you, Ordell? You want your reward money? All you had to do was ask."

"It ain't about the money. It's about this. Can't you feel it, Clint? Can't you feel the blood runnin' through yer veins like wildfire? There ain't nothing like this!"

"So that means you're just crazy, then," Clint said. "I guess I can't say I'm too surprised."

This time, when Ordell spoke, it was from a slightly different angle. "You should take this as a compliment. You're one of the few men to ever draw my blood during one of these excursions. That ain't no small feat."

"Yeah. I'm honored." Clint shifted around the rock a bit, doing his best to keep as much stone between him and Ordell.

"Huntin' wanted men was always good for sport, but they were too easy. They'd been runnin' fer too long and were already tired. Most of 'em wanted to be caught anyhow. This is like a gift, Clint. It makes a man appreciate his life more."

"So if I just thanked you for the lesson and praised my new outlook on life, you'd just let me go?"

There was a few moments of silence before Ordell spoke again. "Nah," he said. "I guess I wouldn't."

After that, another shot from Ordell's rifle blasted through the air. Even though Clint couldn't see a single trace of the hunter, the shot Ordell fired sparked against the rock a few inches from Clint's head. Clint reflexively ducked and scooted around the rock before getting a look at the spot that had been hit.

"You still there, Clint?" Ordell shouted.

Clint bit his tongue and shook his head, cursing himself for playing Ordell's game once more. Even though he didn't have much choice at the moment, he still hated giving the hunter another free shot at him.

Just then, Ordell fired again. This time, however, it wasn't at Clint.

The big rifle sent its round through hanging branches and across the river like the end of a drill. Clint could practically feel the lead pass by, but it was too far off the mark to have been meant for him. He looked in the direction the bullet had gone and was just in time to see a few quick shots fired from that side of the river.

Holding his rifle in front of him, Howlett ran as quickly as he could. His movements made his limp even worse, but he managed to get to where Clint was huddled without falling into the river.

"About time you showed up," Clint said. "I've nearly made enough noise to get myself killed."

"Looks like he nearly got you pegged," Howlett said between breaths.

"Yeah, but he's farther away than I thought," Clint said in a voice that was soft enough to keep from carrying too far.

"How can you tell?"

"The spot where that bullet hit. If he'd been closer, it would have blasted out a bigger piece of rock. This bullet just made a crack."

When Howlett looked at the chipped section of rock, he let out a low whistle and shook his head. "Still looks like a nasty piece of work to me."

"It is."

"How far away you reckon he is?"

"I'd say about a hundred yards across the river."

"A hundred yards?" Howlett grumbled as another shot blazed from across the river.

Not only was this shot closer than the last, but it punched a deeper gouge into the rock.

"Make that about sixty yards now," Clint said.

"Hey there, Howlett," Ordell shouted. "You havin' as much fun as I am?"

"Fuck you!"

Ordell's laughter rolled toward the river and slowly faded away. "Too bad about yer Indian friend. He had some real promise. Or didn't you know about that?"

"What's he talkin' about?" Howlett asked.

"Just what we talked about before. Right now, we need to get out from behind this rock. He's playing with us now, but he'll either force us out when he's ready or he'll chip pieces of this thing away until we're sitting in the open."

"What do you propose we do? We can't even see the bastard!"

"You see those two trees that form a V back there?" Clint asked. "Ordell's got to be in those trees or near them."

"How can you tell?"

"Same way he knew where to aim at us. By the sound of his voice."

"Dammit. My ears must not be what they used to."

"You're going to have to trust me, then," Clint said. "All we need to do is stick to our original plan."

Howlett pulled in a deep breath and got his bad leg beneath him. "Let's go."

FORTY-FOUR

After Ordell took his next shot, Clint bolted away from the rock in one direction and Howlett bolted in another. Since Clint could see that Howlett wasn't moving too well, he turned and started firing that much quicker.

In the back of Clint's mind, he ticked off the seconds it would take for Ordell to reload and fire the rifle. He had it worked out almost perfectly since he'd test-fired the weapon enough times when he was repairing it. Every so often, however, Ordell would get a shot off that was even faster than Clint had predicted.

Howlett stopped trying to move quickly and settled for firing accurately. Even as a few of Ordell's shots came at him, Howlett kept moving at his steady pace while firing again and again into the trees. Every time Ordell shot at him, Howlett was able to get a better idea of where those shots were coming from. Before too long, he could hear heavy steps stamping through the underbrush instead of more rifle shots.

"He's moving!" Howlett shouted.

Having left his rifle at the river, Clint kept his body low and drew his Colt. With his right hand wrapped around the pistol, his left hand took hold of his knife. Clint swung the blade in sweeping moves to clear anything in front of him that might trip him up. He didn't worry about snares or traps along the route he took, because the path had already been scouted and cleared.

Clint heard movement ahead and to the left, so he dug his feet into the ground and moved even faster. The next shot fired from Ordell's rifle thundered through the air loudly enough to set Clint's ears ringing. Since he didn't hear the bullet shred himself or anything else near him, Clint knew that Ordell was still firing at Howlett.

As much as Clint wanted to return fire and buy Howlett a moment to draw a breath, he held off and kept running. He even kept running when he turned off the path and into a section of woods that might have been trapped.

Clint kept swinging his blade, putting absolute faith in his own senses to warn him if anything was about to harm him. His ears were filled with the pounding of his own footsteps and heartbeat. His eyes, on the other hand, caught a very welcome sight.

As Clint raised his Colt to point at Ordell, he saw the hunter straighten up and bring his rifle around. The long weapon may have been powerful and accurate, but it was still unwieldy as hell and slowed Ordell down enough for Clint to take his first shot.

The modified Colt barked once and clipped a piece from Ordell's side.

Grunting and twisting to protect that side, Ordell started backing away from Clint. As he headed for the river, Ordell sighted along his rifle and took a shot.

Clint was still moving and heard the lead thunder through the spot he'd just left. He fired again, but Ordell managed to pull his trigger at the same time, forcing Clint to drop before getting blasted out of his boots. Ordell's round tore through Clint's back as he dropped, sending a fiery pain through his body.

A few cautious movements told Clint that he'd just gotten a flesh wound. Of course, that didn't make it hurt any less. Lifting his arm to fire another shot was painful, but since Ordell was still moving and firing back at him, Clint pushed through the pain pretty quickly.

Following Ordell this far had brought him back around toward the river. Acting on pure reflex, Clint bolted for the water while emptying his pistol in Ordell's direction. When he emerged from the trees, he saw Howlett on one knee fifty yards or so downstream.

Howlett gave Clint a wave and pointed toward the trees.

Clint didn't need to be told Ordell was there. He just hoped to reload before the hunter drew a bead on him.

The next series of shots came from Howlett as he fired and worked his rifle lever at an impressive pace. Soon, he was able to flush Ordell from the trees.

Ordell could barely be seen as he stepped forward and took aim at Howlett. "What the hell's wrong with you?" Ordell shouted. "Didn't you know that Clint killed that Indian friend of yours? I would've thought you'd be glad when I dropped Clint first. In fact, why don't we take Clint down right now and be done with it? We can have ourselves another hunt later if you like. Just between you and me."

From where he stood, Clint could just see a slight rustle of movement in the trees behind Ordell. The only way he saw it at all was because Clint had been expecting it since this whole fight began.

A pair of strong, dark arms wrapped around Ordell. One arm cinched in around Ordell's neck and the other held the sharpened stone blade of a tomahawk under his chin.

"That's where you're wrong," Crow hissed into Ordell's ear.

Ordell's face dropped and the color drained from his skin as he was forced to rethink his belief in ghosts.

Seeing that their own trap had been sprung, Clint and Howlett moved in closer. Clint reloaded his Colt and holstered it while Howlett grabbed the rifle from Ordell's hands. The hunter wasn't about to let it go so easily, but the tomahawk under his chin made Ordell loosen his grip.

"This ain't right," Ordell said. "That Injun was killed. I saw it!"

"You saw me shoot and you saw Crow fall down," Clint explained.

Squirming in Crow's grasp, Ordell asked, "Are you just gonna let them kill me, Clint? You're not that sort! You won't just stand by and watch a man get murdered."

"You mean like I had to watch you murder your own nephew? If you've been counting on me showing you mercy after every time you tried to hunt me down and kill me, then you're sadly mistaken. I'm not in this for the bounty on your head and I'm not in this to execute you. I wanted to make sure your hunting days were over."

From behind Ordell, Crow snarled, "They are over."

"Th . . . this ain't a way to kill a man!" Ordell shouted with desperation shining through every word. "At least give me a weapon and fight me proper!"

"You are no man," Crow said. "You are an animal."

Clint turned his back and walked to the river as the killing blow was struck. After all the running and gunfire, it was a quiet moment followed by the thump of Ordell's body hitting the ground.

FORTY-FIVE

"It is done," Crow said as he stepped up next to Clint and knelt down to wash his tomahawk in the river.

Clint was stooping down to take a drink. Glancing over his shoulder, he caught a glimpse of Ordell's body.

"After all that, I half expected him to jump up and start tearing after us again," Howlett said as he stood next to Crow.

"Not any more," Clint said.

"I suppose you'll be wanting to haul his carcass back to the law since he didn't get his trial."

Clint shrugged. "Actually, I figured he should just be buried out here. It's where he belongs."

"Nah," Howlett grumbled. "You were right before. Them other folks that lost their kin to that bastard need to know it's over. I know Ed Gray's family checks in with the marshal every so often to see what they know about Ed's killer. It's about time they got some good news."

"Good news for them and plenty of other folks," Clint said. "I like the sound of that."

"And I will bring this to my people," Crow said as he held Ordell's rifle reverently. "Seeing this weapon taken from its owner will be very good news to them."

"The best news I've had for a while was knowing you were following through on our plan to trap Ordell," Clint said. "For a moment, I thought you truly were going to attack me."

"I was thinking about it," Crow said.

Walking along the river toward them, Rain rushed over to Crow to give him a hug. "And that is all you'll do. I asked Clint if you were all right and he wouldn't tell me."

Crow let his sister dote on him for a few seconds before pushing her away. "Ordell could have been watching and listening to every word. You knew that."

"I know, but I still worried. I thought Ordell had seen me when I brought Clint's plan to you. I thought he'd seen me when I warned Clint that he was near so you two could start your fight. No matter how careful I was," she said as a chill worked its way down her spine, "he still crept up on me and could have—"

"But he didn't," Clint said. "You did a fine job."

"I second that!" Howlett declared. "Hell, I wouldn't mind if you brought your sister along on a regular basis. She's one of the best scouts I've ever seen."

"Right now, I just want to get out of these woods and go home," Rain told him.

Clint couldn't agree more.

Watch for

THE FRIENDS OF WILD BILL HICKOK

302nd novel in the exciting GUNSMITH series
from Jove

Coming in February!

J GIANT ACTION! GIANT ADVENTURE!

THE GUNSMITH

GIANT

Giant Westerns featuring The Gunsmith

LITTLE SURESHOT AND THE WILD WEST SHOW
0-515-13851-7

DEAD WEIGHT
0-515-14028-7

RED MOUNTAIN
0-515-14206-9

Available wherever books are sold or at
penguin.com

J. R. ROBERTS

THE GUNSMITH

Available wherever books are sold or at penguin.com